me & My Best Friend
Became Adventurers in a
fantasy world!

written by
Terry Bartley

Contents

Chapter One

A Third Option

Growing up as an Orc of the Hukawan tribe, it was drilled into me how much the people of Anglachel feared us. The humans of our tribe could get away with a bit more, but because Orcs were big and scary and different, we had to be very careful within the city. We couldn't avoid it all together, hunting parties had to enter the city to trade furs and leathers for the things our tribe needed that the jungle couldn't provide. The people of Anglachel accepted that small groups of Orcs would briefly enter the city, but they would always travel as a group, do their business, and leave. My father reminded me of this before I joined him for my first trip into the city. This was an important milestone every hunter crosses on their sixteenth birthday.

The Hukawan hunters wear thin leather armor because it takes a lot of flexibility to easily move around the jungle. They all carry bows, arrows, and hand axes. Most hunters tend to favor one weapon or the other. My father, Tanwe, tended to prefer his ax and he has been training me to use it since I was very young. I always liked the way my green skin paired with the light brown armor.

My father had been to the city of Anglachel many times. He had told me about the large buildings, and the delicious aromas drifting out of the windows of restaurants, and the hustle that touched every part of the city. I knew to expect that the city was a much different place from the jungle. I didn't expect to see so many different kinds of people.

I saw the fear I had learned about early on. If I followed the eyes of humans passing us on the street, I noticed that they stopped on the tusks of the adult hunters. I spotted a Halfling mother walking with her two children a couple of blocks ahead of us. Her face tensed when she spotted us and then she hurried her children across the street so they wouldn't have to pass us. Those sorts of moments were frequent enough that it was impossible to miss.

However, what piqued my interest were the children playing together in the open lots where shacks used to be. A Halfling girl, much like the one forced to flee from us earlier, kicked a red ball. It rolled across the dirt and a large boy, a Giant, raced towards it. He scooped up the ball and chased after the girl. She was giggling as she ran between his legs and he bent down to attempt to tag her with the ball. As she emerged on the other side of him, he lost his balance and tumbled to the ground.

"No fair!" His voice boomed throughout the city streets. "You're too little. It is too hard to reach you."

"Shut up, Pyson. You've caught me before. You just have to do better!" The Halfling girl said encouragingly.

Pyson, the Giant boy, reached his massive arm around and grasped the leg of the Halfling girl. She also stumbled and fell to the ground beside him.

"Got you, Tini!" he declared.

"That is cheating, Pyson," she said, laughing and rolling towards Pyson.

"Maybe a little," he said as he turned his head in Tini's direction, also laughing.

I couldn't understand why these children who were so different could play together without fear, when everyone was so terrified of people like me. Tini began to stand up and dust herself off when she noticed me staring at them.

"Hi! Do you want to play with us?" she said, sounding so innocent. She didn't realize that she was supposed to be scared of me. It felt nice. I knew I couldn't stay. I turned to continue walking with the hunting party, butthey were gone. I was so distracted watching them play that I'd lost the hunting party.

"I'm sorry, I have to go," I shouted across the street to Tini and ran down the sidewalk.

"It's o.k. We can play later!" Pyson said, sitting up.

It made me a little sad to know that I never could. I waved in their general direction as I sprinted down the block to find my father's hunting party. I stopped at the corner and looked in every direction and I couldn't see them anywhere. I looked down the sidewalk on all four sides and they looked the same. A dirty, concrete sidewalk littered with garbage while grass grew in between the individual slabs of rock. I turned left, because I wouldn't have to cross the street and I knew I had to keep moving. I could probably get out of the city on my own, but I was terrified of what would happen if someone with authority recognized me as an Orc in the city by herself.

As I began walking down the block, I started to hear muffled sniffling. I looked down an alley as I passed and I could hear the sound more clearly. I stalked down the alley, following the cries. I approached a discarded chair and moved it to the side. My locked eyes with a terrified Goblin child that looked to be about the same age as me.

The Goblin had yellow-green skin and wore gray wolf furs crafted into a shirt and pants, featuring buttons made of chestnut shells. He was in a seated fetal position, hugging his knees against his chest. His hair was a very pale yellow, but with vibrant blue and red streaks running through it, tied into a high ponytail. I knew there were tribes with goblins in the jungle, but I'd never seen one up close.

"I don't want to hurt you," I said, showing the goblin both of my hands.

"Promise?" They managed to say through tears.

"Promise," I agreed. I placed one of my palms on my chest and held the other facing the Goblin. This was the symbol of swearing an oath of our goddess, Estel. I know the goblins in the jungle worshiped the same goddess and I hoped they had similar traditions. The Goblin mimicked my motions and touched their palm to mine. Their face began to relax a bit.

"I'm Karuk," I introduced myself. "What are you doing all alone in the city?"

I knew Goblins had similar rules to Orcs. They also only entered the city in groups.

"You won't tell?" they asked. I couldn't help it, I let out a laugh. "What? What's so funny?" they asked.

"Who would I tell?" I asked. "We're here by ourselves."

"Oh, right," they remembered. "My name is Gin. I snuck into the city."

I was impressed that it would even occur to a Goblin this young to sneak into the city. I wouldn't have dared to come here by myself. I was too afraid of what would happen. It must have shown on my face because Gin's mouth crept into a grin.

"You don't think I'm crazy?" he asked.

"No. Well, maybe a little," I admitted. " But I'm mostly curious. Why would you want to come here by yourself?"

"The music," he said simply.

"What music?" I inquired.

"I heard Goblins talking about how people played music in taverns. I love to play music with my tribe, but I get tired of the same thing all the time. I wanted to hear something new," Gin explained.

I never really cared for the music of my people, so I couldn't understand risking my life to hear a new song. But I could relate to getting tired of what life in the jungle had to offer. I basically had two options. I could be a hunter, like my father, and join the hunting parties. Or I could become a domestic worker, like my mother. I could stay at the settlement and process the animal pelts, cook the food, and prepare for religious ceremonies. All my life, I knew that doing one of those two things would be my destiny. I couldn't help but wonder if there could be a third option. I never dared speak it, because I worried the tribe would think I was ungrateful. But, still, I wondered.

"I get it," I empathized.

"Really? You'll help me?" Gin said, presuming I already understood what exactly he was asking of me. I considered the look of excitement on his face and I couldn't stand to be the reason it faltered.

"Sure," I agreed. "Let's go listen to some music."

"Woohoo!" he exclaimed, jumping into the air and revealing the small drum slung across his body. I quickly ran to look down the road, making sure no one heard. It looked like we were safe.

"Try to keep it down," I whispered. "If we're going to travel through the city, we can't let any adults see us. They'd probably arrest us, or kill us, or something."

"I know," Gin said meekly. "Sorry."

"You can be excited," I advised. "Just do it quietly."

"Woohoo!" he whispered, slightly raising his fist into the air.

"That's better." I said with a slight giggle in my voice.

"So where are we going?".

"To a tavern, to listen to music. Didn't I tell you that?" he asked

"I know that, Gin. Where is the tavern?" I asked.

"Oh, I don't know. We have to find it," he said, as though it was the easiest thing in the world.

"You mean I'll have to find it," I said, reaffirming what he meant.

"Yeah, what'd I say?" he asked.

"O.K.," I said. "I think I might know where to start."

I led Gin down the way I'd come and walked over to the open lot where I saw Pyson and Tini playing earlier.

"You came back to play with us!" Tini exclaimed upon seeing me.

"Not right now," I explained. "My friend and I were actually looking for a tavern. Do you know where one is?"

"I do! My mommy took me to one a few days ago for breakfast. We had eggs with cheese and bacon. It was really good!" she said.

"Do you know if they play music there?" Gin asked.

"I think so. There was a big stringed instrument on a stage. It was bigger than me!" Tini said.

"Bigger than me?" Pyson asked curiously.

"A little bit," Tini said.

"That's funny," Pyson replied, laughing.

"It is!" Tini said, joining in his laughing fit.

Gin and I started laughing too. I didn't fully understand why, but it was fun. We calmed down about a few seconds later.

"So you know how to get there?" I asked.

"Yes!" Tini said defiantly. "You go down that way one block, then you turn right and walk for three blocks, then you turn right again and walk two blocks."

"Thank you!" I said.

"You're welcome. What are your names?" Tini asked.

"I'm Karuk," I said. She grabbed my hand and started shaking it.

Pyson picked up Gin and held his little Goblin body even with his face.

"And you are?" he asked.

"I'm Gin," he said as the giant pulled him in for a bear hug.

"See you later!" Tini said, waving her arm above her head. Pyson gently set Gin down and did the same.

"Bye!" Gin said as I began pulling him down the street.

We followed Tini's directions, and I was heartened to see the sun was beginning to set. We'd be a lot harder to notice as an Orc and a Goblin without the sun shining down on us. I kept us close to the buildings, and we moved at a slow pace so we wouldn't draw attention. Tini's directions weren't perfect, but I could tell we were getting close when we started to hear music ahead of us.

"That's it!" Gin excitedly whispered. He tugged on me to pull me down the street. He headed for the front door, and I pulled him past it.

"What are you doing? It's right there!" Gin complained.

"We can't just walk through the front door. We'll get caught!" I reiterated.

Gin looked annoyed, but he understood. We walked around to the other side of the building and saw an open window around the back. There weren't any doors on this side and it faced the wall between the city and the jungle.

"Hey! This is close to the hole I snuck through!" Gin exclaimed.

"Good, we can sneak out after we listen for a bit," I said.

We sat down under the window and leaned against the building. As the music drifted through the window, Gin looked like the happiest person I'd ever seen in my life. He tapped out a rhythm on the edge of his drum. It wasn't too loud, but he got to feel like he was playing along.

I didn't expect to get anything out of this. As I said, music has never really been my thing. But then I started listening to the lyrics. They were singing songs about people going on adventures. There was a song about a woman who had been kidnapped by a Troll and she fought her way out. Another song told of a human man and a Gnome woman that traveled through the hells and outsmarted a Demon lord to save their village. Then my mind was completely blown when I heard a song about an Orc woman named Tadarin who had rushed through the barrier between Anglachel and "The Jungle of Despair," which I guess is what they call the jungle here. Anyway, she ran through the barrier and single-handedly battled a Dragon that had swooped down to attack the city. They considered her a hero! An Orc hero!

After we finished listening to the musicians for the night, I walked with Gin to the hole he'd snuck through and helped him through it. We promised to meet up at a clearing between our settlements next week to sneak in and listen to music again. I crept along the edge of the wall until I spotted the guards at the gate into the jungle. I'd gotten there right in time. I could see my father talking to a guard. I figured he was asking about me. I slipped around the street and joined the other Orcs in the back of the hunting party. I could hear what my father was saying now.

"We just want to look around for her a little bit longer. Could you just let the town guards know what we're doing?" he asked tentatively.

"I'm sorry, sir," the guard said, hand on the hilt of his sword. "We can't let Orcs remain in the city at night. That's the law."

I walked up to my father and tugged on his fur cloak. He looked down and a huge grin spread across his fac e."Karuk! You're here!" he exclaimed.

"I was in the back," I lied.

"We're good sir," he said, turning back to the guard. "We can leave now."

"Thank you," the guard said, relieved. "I'm sure neither of us wanted any trouble."

I crossed through the gate with the hunting party, thinking about the songs I'd heard that evening. For the first time, I started to feel like I knew what I wanted to do when I grew up. I wanted to be an adventurer.

Chapter Two

Don't Call It That

"Praise to Estel, the great goddess of balance. She, who uprooted the evils away from our lands and gave our people the ability to thrive." The large fire in the center of the tent flared as the old Shaman threw powder into it. They waved their spiritual stick above their head, dried jungle fruits hanging off of it. They were human with long gray hair, and skin the color of a mountain range at sunset. The Hukawan tribe, a collection of humans and Orcs, gathered in the large ceremonial tent in the center of the village at the ending of every week.

"Praise to the trees, the soil and the animals that sustain us. Praise to the balance of nature that allows all creatures to live alongside one another," they continued.

I stood up with the rest of my tribe as we began to wave our hands above our heads. I've started every day just like this for as long as I can remember. I was nineteen years old at the time and I appreciated being a part of something bigger than myself, but I also wanted more than the life the tribe could provide. I wanted to be like Tadarin and all the other heroes Gin and I had heard about for the past three years. I was beginning to grow tired of preserving my culture in exchange for never leaving. I needed to get out.

"What do you mean, you want to leave?" my mother incredulously asked the first time I'd brought it up just after that first encounter with Gin.

"I just don't know if I want to be a hunter or a domestic tribesman for the rest of my life. What if I want to live in Anglachel, and just work an office job or something?" I sheepishly asked.

"Karuk, my dear girl, you are an Orc of the Hukawan tribe. Who would hire you in Anglachel? You know that they are scared of us," she concluded.

Sadly, I knew she was right. I always saw the way the people of the city looked at us. I knew there was no place for me in the city.

But that doesn't mean I didn't crave it. I found myself feeling envious of the human children born in our tribe. They had options that simply were not available to me.

After the morning ceremony, I hid within the crowd so I could sneak out of the village without my family noticing. Once I made it into the open jungle, I raced through the trees, jumping over roots and swinging across branches. Some of my earliest memories were racing against adult hunters across the jungle. I always had a knack for finding my way through the wilds. I noticed the way this branch curved upward, or how those roots spread out a little farther. I may have wanted to leave the tribe, but I still loved the jungle.

I made it to a clearing beside the large waterfall. I'd been coming here for the past three years and it was the only place I could drop my mask and fantasize about the life I truly wanted. This was the place I could truly be myself.

I heard Gin approach before I saw him. His drumbeat carried throughout the trees and I could hear the birds singing along. He danced his way into the clearing, lost in the music. Gin's thin, muscular arms beat a rhythm more appropriate in an Anglachel tavern than in the middle of the Jungle. His yellow-green skin, the color of an unripened lime, shone in the sunlight. Sweat dripped off of his pointed nose and ears. As he finished his song, I offered a hearty applause.

"Stop it, stop it," Gin said. "It is only us here. You can just say thank you for the private concert. You know, I should charge you for this."

"Of course," I replied, grinning at him, "What sort of game would you like for payment? Boars seem to be plentiful this time of year."

He gave me an unsatisfied look.

"Oh, you wanted coin?" I asked sarcastically. "I'm afraid an Orc of the Hukawan tribe has no use for it."

Gin unstrapped the drum from his shoulder and collapsed into a nearby moss pile. "I know that's not true."

I followed his lead and sat on a log from a recently fallen tree. "Maybe so, but where would I get it?"

"I keep telling you, Ruki. We need to go to the city. I could play at a tavern and earn us some money. You know I'm good enough," Gin said.

"You're no doubt good enough. I've never seen anyone so skilled with an instrument that they can call upon magic without a ritual," I said. "But how would we get past the guards? They would never let either of us enter the city alone, much less together. The only way an Orc or a Goblin can get into the city is with a trade party. And there's no way we could sneak away without getting ourselves killed."

"You can stop being practical any time now," Gin begged.

"It is a nice fantasy," I offered.

"It is that."

I swung my legs onto the log and began to lay down. Just as I started to lounge, I heard the scream. A distinctly masculine voice from somewhere down the river. I launched out of my seated position to grab a vine hanging from the trees above. I scrambled up the vine so I could get a better view of whoever it was from above.

I squinted my eyes to better focus in the distance. I could see a river boat, clearly of Anglachelan make, careening towards the waterfall at an accelerating speed.

As it got closer, I could see a panicky, tall, young human. He had shoulder-length, unkempt chestnut-blonde hair, and wore a long black trench coat. He was running from one side of the boat to the other. He screamed again, and this time I could just make out what he was saying.

"Help! Someone, please! Help me!"

I lept into action, making my way down to the river by swinging from alternating vines. I couldn't dive in. His boat was too big, and if I was to have any chance at stopping it, I had to use the leverage of standing on the ground provided. But his boat was too far out for me to reach him.

"Quick, give me a platform," I called out to Gin.

He sprung up and threw his drum around his shoulder in a singular motion. He quickly began beating out a driving rhythm. A solid pink force field appeared, jutting out of the river bank. I easily lowered myself onto the force field and it began to blink out. I had to jump to avoid crashing into the rapid river. The force field reappeared as I came back down.

"Sorry about that," Gin wailed, "I've never had to use these for anything practical before."

"You're fine, just try to keep it steady," I instructed.

Now that the surface began to feel a bit more sturdy, I drew my hunting ax from my belt. I had constructed it from my tribe's ancestral steel trees—the strongest wood that I knew of. As long as I could keep hold of it, it wouldn't break. As the boat raced past, I thrust my ax into it. It was a solid swing and it stuck. It tugged hard on me, but I was able to ground myself on the pink force field. I slowly walked it back to the river bank.

The human ran to the back side of the boat and shouted, "Ve Ex To!"

The river still beat against the boat, but the pull decreased. I eased it to a stop, getting off of the pink force field; the human and I took a deep breath. His golden rectangular glasses fogged a bit.

"Thank you, thank you so much!" he said, lifting his head. A startled look appeared on his face as it tilted towards us.

"Don't worry," I assured, "Neither of us intends to hurt you. That would have been a lot of effort to save someone just so we could kill them."

That didn't reassure him.

"Not that that's the only reason we wouldn't kill you. Goblins and Orcs aren't actually as aggressive as everyone says," Gin continued. "I'm Gin. This is Karuk. Her friends call her Ruki."

That seemed to do the trick. The young man began to ease his shoulders a bit.

"They do not," I whirled on Gin. "You're the only person that calls me that, and you can only get away with it because we've been friends for so long."

A smile began to creep onto the human's face.

"M-my name is Dara," the human piped up. "Dara MacCarthy."

"Nice to meet you," I returned. I extended my hand towards him and realized I hadn't sheathed my hunting ax. I quickly tucked it back into my belt. Gin had sauntered up and offered his hand before Dara could notice my mistake.

"You as well," Dara said. "Sorry if I was impolite earlier. I was just surprised to see an Orc and a Goblin together. I had always heard that your tribes hated each other."

"No, we like each other," Gin replied.

"I'd more say 'tolerate,'" I explained. "My tribe, the Hukawan, stay on this side of this river. Gin's tribe stays on the other side. In the centuries our tribes existed, we found it works better for everyone. There's always enough resources to share."

Dara nodded, as if he was considering this. "That makes sense."

"And we're not all Orcs. The Hukawan are both Orcs and humans," I said.

"Yeah, yeah, yeah," Gin interrupted. "And Goblins live with Halflings. Everyone knows that. You don't need to bore our new friend to death already."

Dara gave a light laugh.

"She does this," Gin stage whispered to him.

"No, no, it is fine," Dara stated. "It is actually exciting to learn something new. I don't think it is common knowledge in Anglachel that there are indigenous humans and Halflings in the Jungle of Despair."

"Please don't call it that," I corrected. "We let you people say that because it keeps you all out. But we just call it The Jungle."

"Of course, of course," Dara apologized. "I'm so sorry."

I didn't want to scare him, but it was admittedly humorous to trip him up socially. "You're good."

"So what brings a scrawny human like you out into The Jungle?" Gin asked.

"It's like I said. I wanted to learn something new. I was a student at Arcana University and I felt like I had learned everything they had to teach me. I thought I'd strike out on my own into The Jungle. My boat got out of control when I tried to tap into the potent elemental magic here."

"That checks out," I said. "Our shaman has said that the magic is nearly uncontrollable here. But we don't know anything about the different flavors of magic. Is that what you call them?"

"Disciplines, but yes. I have actually never seen anyone tap into barrier magic the way you did, Gin. What kind of training do you have?" Dara inquired.

"I wouldn't say I have training. I've just always been really tuned into music and anytime I play I've been able to create pink force fields. I don't know what that is," Gin admitted.

"That sounds similar to sorcerers, people that are born with the ability to tap into a specific discipline of magic. But I've never seen it require music. I would be very interested to study that," Dara suggested.

"Sure."

While they were talking I took a moment to assess our surroundings to make sure we were safe. The reason Gin and I liked meeting here is that it is a pretty open area with fewer trees than the rest of the jungle. While we're here, most of the animals stay away because they don't want to be spotted. All I could hear were the sounds of the babbling river and insects buzzing around.

"So you were just planning on living in the Jungle?" Gin asked.

"Oh no, not at all. I want to travel the world. I actually have a checklist of all of the different geographic regions in Galevyn," Dara excitedly explained.

I turned around at the mention of a new word. "Galevyn?"

"That is what we call the planet we live on, in Anglachel. And in the rest of the world, as far as I knew," Dara said quizzically.

"Really? We always just called it 'Earth.' Because, ya' know, dirt," Gin responded.

Dara reached into a bag hanging off of his shoulder and pulled out a quill and a small notebook. He whispered something into the feather and began scribbling something down. "Wow," Dara exclaimed. "I guess it is a totally different world out here. So exciting!"

We stood there in awkward silence for a moment, looking at each other. I don't think we knew what we were supposed to do next. Gin and I have never spoken to a magic student before. Dara had surely not spoken to an Orc or a Goblin before.

"So you said you wanted to travel?" Gin finally asked.

"Yes," Dara said. "Once I get my boat to the sea, I can use some minor transmutation magic to turn it into something that can get me across it." Dara paused and considered his beached boat on the river bank. "But I don't know how I'll get it there," he said, seemingly noticing for the first time. "I guess I have to go back to town already. Everyone's going to make fun of me."

This sounded a little bit like an adventure and maybe an opportunity for Gin and I to start figuring a path out of The Jungle.

"I could help," I chimed in.

"Yeah?" Dara asked. "You'd do that for a person you just met? That's so nice."

"I never said I was doing anything for free," I said directly, folding my arms.

"My coin is pretty limited," he began.

"No, don't pay in coin!" Gin said. I glared at him. What was he doing? We needed this coin to get out. "You can pay us by letting us go with you!"

"That's fine with me," Dara said. "After seeing the two of you handle yourselves earlier, you could be very useful to have around."

"One moment," I interjected. I grabbed Gin by his arm and dragged him far enough to be out of Dara's earshot.

"What are you talking about?" I demanded. "We can't just go. We have to plan. We have to pack. We haven't even said goodbye to our families."

"Do you really think your mom or dad will just let you go if you told them? I don't know about your tribe, but I've heard stories of Goblins thrown in cages by their brethren because they were saying crazy things like going into the city alone."

"No, I have heard those, too. Our people's position with the city is so precarious, they can't risk anyone messing everything up," I remembered.

"Yeah, that's right," Gin smugly said. "How many chances are we going to get like this? A magic human showed up, WITH a friggin' boat? I've got my drum, you have your ax. We have everything we need. How is that not a sign? We have to go with him."

I considered his words for a moment. I'd spent my whole life praising Estel, the goddess of balance. In a way, this may be the only way Gin and I could get away from our tribes. After two centuries of Orcs and Goblins being stuck in this jungle, maybe this is tipping the balance for our people. Even if only slightly.

And Gin is right. As much as I want to say goodbye to my tribe, my parents, they'd never understand and they wouldn't just let me go. If we really wanted to leave The Jungle, really leave, this might be our only chance. I looked back towards my village before deciding.

After a beat, I dragged Gin back to Dara.

"I can walk, ya' know," Gin complained.

I looked Dara in the eyes. "We will go with you."

"Cool!" Dara said. "So are you going to carry this boat by yourself or . . . ."

"I can handle one side. The two of you are going to have to try to hold the other side up so it doesn't drag," I instructed.

"I'm a musician, Ruki," Gin said. "I don't really do manual labor."

"What am I getting myself into?" I asked myself aloud as I picked up the front end of the boat.

Chapter Three

Swimming Through the Storm

WE HAD ONLY JUST started drifting into the open sea when the storm became a problem. It doesn't often storm in The Jungle, but when it does, it pours. And apparently, the weather gets way more extreme out on the sea. It became very clear to me very quickly that Dara had no idea how to captain a ship, let alone steer it in these conditions. It was all we could do to stay afloat and on the deck.

"Any ideas, wizard man?" Gin screamed over the sheets of rain.

Dara struggled as the boat shook in the waves. "Hold out until morning and then find our bearings?"

"You want us to keep fighting this storm all night without knowing if we're even making any progress?" I questioned. Judging by the looks on Gin and Dara's faces, they knew I had no intention of doing that.

Dara held his hand over his face to block out the rain and looked up. "If I could see the stars, I could figure out what way is south. But I can't see anything through these clouds."

"I'll figure it out." I decided, after considering our situation and realizing that something had to change if we were going to make it. Gin and I were not going to run away from our families just to die out here.

I dove off the boat and into the sea. I could hear shouts from Gin and Dara, but they didn't matter right now. I knew that we were never going to figure out what direction to head from out here, but I knew that I could always find my way around The Jungle. The shoreline hadn't quite faded from view yet, and I furiously swam towards it. It wasn't easy swimming through the storm, but my Orcish body was built for this kind of thing. I just kept going until I reached land. I don't know how long it actually took, but every muscle in my body was screaming.

My hand finally landed on a muddy patch at the bottom of a plateau facing the sea. I remembered passing it when we had started the journey. I began climbing the rock face and pushed the pain into the back of my mind. I didn't have time to worry about that right now. I just kept pulling myself up the shale until I reached the top.

Once there, I surveyed my surroundings. I used to come out to this cliff to watch the ocean after a long day of hunting. I saw the pair of trees that led to the deer trail I could follow to the outskirts of my settlement. I mentally followed the trail and considered where the settlement would be in relation to this cliff. I pointed my palm straight in front of me and traced where I would be. When I ended at the edge of my home, my hand was facing sharply to the left of where I'd started. I knew the settlement was due north of the river we'd taken to reach the sea.

I kept my hand where it was, and I turned my head to see the boat. I could see them in the distance, a speck, but a speck that was clearly facing in a north western direction. If we traveled that way all night, we'd probably end back up on the opposite side of The Jungle. That wouldn't be helpful. We would have to adjust the boat about 120 degrees east to travel to the south. I looked around to see if there was anything on the jungle floor I could use once I'd made it back. I spotted a thick, long vine. I sliced about four squares of it with my hand ax and wrapped it around my shoulder like a sash, tying it in front. Then I took a deep breath and dove back into the water.

I was once again swimming through the storm, but I kept my eyes on the speck of a boat I saw in the distance. It gradually became bigger and bigger; then, finally, I could hear welcoming shouts from my compatriots.

"Ruki!" Gin exclaimed. "You're back!" Then he slapped me across the face as I was climbing back onto the boat. It didn't hurt, he's a little guy, after all. "Never do that again. I'm not doing this without you. We never leave each other."

I toppled onto the deck, but I looked Gin in the eyes.

"Sorry, Gin, you're right. We never leave each other," I agreed.

"Why did you do that?" Dara asked. "What were you trying to do?"

"I figured out which way we need to go," I stated matter-of-factly.

I pulled myself up, and I gestured in the direction we needed to turn the vessel.

"I'm impressed," Dara said instinctively. "That was insane. But I'm impressed."

"Is there a way to block the wind so we can try to, I don't know, paddle that way?" I asked both of them.

"I could play a barrier around the sails," Gin suggested.

"And I can create wind. If we can block out the other wind, I can produce wind in whatever direction we need to go," Dara said.

"You're gonna have to help me, Ruki," Gin said, looking at me with pleading eyes. "It is real hard to play in this storm."

"I know what to do," I concluded.

I unlashed the vine from around my shoulder, and I tied it around Gin's waist. I pulled it taut and braced myself to keep him in place. Dara positioned himself directly behind the sail, and Gin began to beat a rhythm into his drum. A sort of pink tent appeared, protecting Dara and the sails from the surrounding storm. I could see he was reciting something, but I couldn't hear it through the whipping winds around us. He pulled a modest candle from his coat, produced a tiny flame on the end of his index finger, and lit the wick. He closed his eyes and held his hand in a southerly direction. He blew out the candle, and the boat jerked, fighting against the waves to move us closer to either Ronan or Ferreria, the countries across the sea to the south of The Jungle. We didn't know where we were headed, but we had absolutely begun our lives as adventurers. Gin continued to play his drum but looked at me with a huge smile on his face. I returned it. It was really happening.

Chapter Four

Following the Dirt Road

WE ENDED UP ON a pebble beach on the northern shore of Ronan. Past the beach, we could see rolling green hills extending into the distance. Growing up in The Jungle, the amount of open land was shocking. It felt unnatural to see so much green space without trees around.

"So what now?" Gin asked.

We all looked at each other expectantly. The ten seconds that followed felt like ten minutes.

Gin looked at both of us incredulously. "Really? No one has thought about the next part?"

"I don't know if you noticed, but we were all a little busy keeping the boat afloat to consider next steps," I reminded him.

"Come on, Ruki," Gin pleaded. "We've been thinking of this day our whole lives! You've gotta have some idea of what you visualized. After we left home to become adventurers, we . . . ." He paused expectantly.

"Why are you looking at me? You were there, too," I argued.

"Don't do this, Ruki. Don't you start blaming me," Gin preemptively defended.

I've always loved Gin. That charming Goblin kept me sane through most of my childhood, but sometimes childhood friends know exactly how to push your buttons. I was tired, I was lost in a new place, and Gin was getting on my last nerve. I could feel myself breathing heavily and I'm sure my face looked as mad as I felt.

"O.K., O.K.," Dara mediated. "Guys, we just landed. We're exhausted. Let's try to find a town and rest. I still have a little coin to get us a room and a meal at a tavern."

"That's it, a tavern!" Gin remembered excitedly. "I can play there for extra money, and we can find adventuring work!"

"That sounds like a plan," I groggily concurred. "And I didn't even have to come up with it. Should we just start walking until we find a road?"

"Yeah, shouldn't take long," Dara responded. "I've read that Ronan is known to have many small villages scattered throughout it. One writer joked that you can't throw a rock without hitting one."

Gin picked up a pebble from the beach and chucked it. Gin is lean and muscular, but it's all for aesthetics. He is not built for strength. The pebble landed among its rocky compatriots further down the beach. "False," Gin declared.

I rolled my eyes. "Just start walking."

It turns out Dara was right. Once we reached the top of the first grassy hill, we saw a dirt road below. I took a moment to appreciate the view. There was a sea of green as far as the eye could see. It was stunning. We turned right on the long stretch of road and walked for about twenty minutes. We eventually saw a wooden sign emblazoned with bright red lettering that read, "Welcome to Éindí Grá!"

Éindí Grá, I would come to find out in the coming weeks, was a typical quaint Ronan village. The dirt road continued into the town and ran down the length of it. We saw a provision store, a doctor's office, a number of small houses, and a tavern. The tavern in this town was called Cabbage and Ale, as evidenced by the hand-painted wooden sign that featured a tankard of ale beside a steaming bowl. My tribe occasionally traded for ale, but I had never actually eaten cabbage before. It must not be native to the jungle.

"Ruki! It's really happening!" Gin excitedly said to me. His delight eroded some of of my weariness away.

"We're becoming adventurers!" I agreed, and a smile crept onto my face. The reality of our dreams coming true was too thrilling to deny.

I noticed Dara had been nervously twirling a gold coin between his fingers. "I just hope they accept Anglachelan gold."

The streets were pretty barren, it felt a little like a ghost town. I was basing that entirely on descriptions I had heard of ghost towns in tavern songs. But there were signs of life. There were large buckets with ladles hanging from a rope that occupied the porches of a number of houses. Fruit pies were sitting on windowsills to cool.

We entered the Cabbage and Ale, and I was struck with a whiff of home. In our settlement, the most prominent smell was always the burnt smell that came with the large fire we used to cook group meals. I was starting to regret leaving without telling anyone goodbye. The Cabbage and Ale featured a prominent fireplace in the center of its modest dining room.

"Give us a moment," a heavily accented matronly voice called our way. "We're only just gettin' past our

lunch rush. Have yeself a seat and we'll be with ye short-
ly."

A chubby Gnome woman with a thicket of red-
dish-gray curls on top of her head stood behind the
bar. The bar top was surprisingly short, though that
made perfect sense when considering the size of the
proprietor. The majority of the tables were also the
same kind of compact, but there were a couple of medi-
um-sized tables near the back corner of the establishment. Dara, Gin, and I seated ourselves as the Gnome
woman walked into a room behind the bar. We sat quietly and took in the comfortable, inviting space around
us.

A moment later, a much younger Gnome woman
came out of a back room. She carried a stool in one
hand and a notepad in the other. She was presumably
some kind of related to the first woman, based on their
similar facial features. Conversely, her curls flowed onto
both of her shoulders in a waterfall of vibrant red. She
wore a white collared tunic sloppily tucked into her
form-fitting leather pants. She placed the stool in front
of our table and stepped onto it with the precision of
someone who had been doing this for most of their life.

"Mam said there was some tall folk here," she began.

"Yes, we were wondering. Where is everyone? The
streets are empty," Dara asked.

The girl laughed to herself "Oh, you lot must not be farmers. They're all working the fields. That's what ye do in the mornin'."

That made a lot of sense. We had farmland in The Jungle, but I was always a hunter. Gathering crops was never one of my responsibilities. I could remember when I was very young, and I'd see my mother walking into the settlement with a basket full of vegetables and herbs. I put my elbow on the table and rested my head on my hand. I didn't want anyone to see the tears that had started to well up at the thought of home.

"What can I get ye?"

"What would someone so beautiful as yourself recommend?" Gin asked in a flirtatious tone.

"Oh, I didn see ye back there," she laughed. "So ye guys have a lil' one with you, too. I thought ye were a child or somethin'."

That properly took the wind out of Gin's sails. A grin crept onto my face, realizing how nice it was to see someone else deflate him.

"Don't mind my friend," I apologized. "We would appreciate a recommendation though. We're not from around here."

"Oh, ye don't have to tell me," she responded. "We don't get many Orcs or Goblins around these parts. Our special is the stew bubblin' over the fire. That's never a bad choice."

"Then give us three of those," Dara answered. "And some water would be great."

"I'll get ye guys some ale," the waitress said.

Gin and I hadn't been to anything even slightly resembling a restaurant, so we were grateful that Dara had ordered for us. The stew was like nothing I had ever tasted before. The broth was a deep brown color and very salty. There were chunks of tender meat that weren't like the game I had eaten back in the jungle. It was also loaded with vegetables. There was a pale green, leafy vegetable that I gathered was Cabbage and Ale's namesake. There were also carrots, potatoes, and fibrous tiny green half-moons. It was delicious, or at least it was so different from anything I had ever eaten before that my brain processed it as delicious. While we ate, we began discussing our next moves.

"So, what do you guys want to do?" Dara asked.

In hindsight, it was surprising that Dara hadn't thought any of this through. He must have wanted to get away from wherever he was coming from as much as we did.

"I want to play here!" Gin exclaimed. "I bet these Ronan Gnomes know how to get down!"

"I meant how do we want to find our first adventure," Dara clarified.

I glanced around the tavern and didn't see any jobs posted. All the songs said that adventurers got jobs from a wanted board. I was confused.

"I thought there were supposed to be jobs posted somewhere in here."

"That's more for big cities," Dara explained. "In small towns like this, everyone basically already knows what's going on. If someone needs help, they just ask their neighbor."

"Just like back home, Ruki," Gin said. "I guess other people aren't that different."

I hated when he got overly saccharine. "Yeah, very sweet, I guess. But that doesn't help us now. We want to be adventurers! We have to have something to do for it to count as an adventure."

"Maybe somewhere around here there's someone who needs help and would be willing to pay?" Dara suggested.

"I've got it!" Gin said, jumping onto his seat. His small Goblin legs standing on the chair brought us face-to-face. "I'll play here tonight, then you guys can ask around with the huge crowd I'll bring in."

"I don't know if we can count on that," I began.

"That's right, Ruki! It is a great idea!" Gin agreed with the version of me he had conjured in his head.

"Is he o.k.?" Dara asked.

"Yeah, you'll get used to it. Sometimes Gin gets an idea and nothing we say can pull it out of there. He just has to do it. It looks like we're waiting until nightfall," I said, accepting our fate.

"That's fine," Dara said. "We need to rest anyway. I'll get us a couple of rooms."

There was only one room available at the Cabbage and Ale. Apparently, it was some sort of Gnomish holiday and a lot of people were in visiting family. To be honest, I had always thought that when Gin and I made our great escape, I'd never look back. I had spent years accepting that I would never see my tribe again. It was comforting to realize that other cultures left home and came back for visits. That sounded nice.

Gods, I needed to shake this homesickness. Why couldn't I just enjoy doing the thing I've always wanted to do?

Our room was Gnome-sized, so Dara and I let Gin have the bed. We both curled up on opposite sides of the room.

"Ruki," I heard his whisper from the bed.

"I'm trying to sleep, Gin," I complained.

"I just wanted to say, that I'm glad we could do this together. I talk a big game, but I would have never had the nerve to leave without you. Thanks for sticking by the weird Goblin that wanted to play music."

While he was being very sweet, it was also undeniably sappy. I would usually call him out for it, but I let him have this one.

"Thanks for sticking by the Orc who wanted to be a hero. I'm glad you're here, too," I said.

"Gods, Ruki, don't be such a sap," Gin teased.

I don't know how long we slept, but the window outside looked very dark by the time we began to stir. I was awoken by Gin springing out of bed and forgetting that I was sleeping beside it on the floor. It didn't hurt, he was so small, after all, but before I could say anything he was already bolting for the door.

"Where's the fire?" I sleepily asked him.

"I don't want to miss the crowd," he said quickly. "This is my first time playing in a real tavern. I don't want to mess it up!"

He ran out the door and closed it behind him. I looked to the other side of the room, and it looked like Dara was in a similar state.

He blearily opened his eyes. "Was that Gin?"

"Yeah, he's chasing his dreams," I yawned.

"Good for him," Dara said. "Do we have to get up and go watch him?"

"Have you never had friends before?" I laughed.

That brought a smile to his face. "Is that a real question? I'm a dorky wizard, of course, I didn't have friends."

"Aren't most wizards dorky?"

"Much to my surprise, they are not. I was hoping I'd find my people at Arcana University, but it was just a different kind of cool kid that excluded me."

I started pushing myself off the floor. "I know we've only known you a couple of days, but I'm pretty sure you found your people. Let's go support Gin."

We took our time getting ready and washing up in the water basin in our room. When we opened the door, I heard a completely different atmosphere than the one we'd walked into. There was a cacophony of voices coming out of the dining room. Dara and I walked out and stood out like sore thumbs. The place was packed with Gnomess. They all were about waist high on the two of us. I felt like a Giant. I spotted Gin, it wasn't hard from way up here. He was frantically talking to the old lady who was the proprietor of this establishment. I tried to walk over to him without literally stepping over the other customers. That felt rude somehow.

"Please! This is the first real tavern I've ever been to. I need to play!" Gin said when I caught up to him.

"If you must," the elderly Gnome relented. "But you better be good. Your room will cost you more if you run these folks out."

"I don't think you have to worry," Gin confident-ly replied, winking at the woman as he walked away. Was he flirting with this old woman? Gods, I hope this doesn't become a thing with him now that we've left The Jungle.

Dara had claimed the "tall folk" table that we had sat in earlier. I gladly joined him. I was not about to continue towering over these Gnomes. Gin found an open corner on the opposite side of the tavern. He began beating a driving rhythm on his drum. I saw dozens of red-colored heads turn in his direction.

"Hello everyone, my name is Gin," he shouted over his playing. "Are you all ready to have a good time tonight?"

The crowd erupted in applause. I had never seen my friend happier. Suddenly all of my concerns faded away. This was the right choice.

The Gnomish crowd loved Gin's music. That was a relief. I always appreciated his talent, but the only real audience he had played for was his Goblin tribe, and from what I hear, that didn't go well. His catchy beats may not suit his kinsman, but they were perfect for these Gnomes tearing up the dance floor.

"Do ye need anything?" The young waitress from before said. She had snuck up on us, or it was just crowded, and we didn't notice.

"I'm good for now," I replied.

"You love him, don't ye?" she asked.

I felt my cheeks turning red, and I felt flustered. "No. Dara and I have just met. We're not together," I said.

"I meant the Goblin. Ye keep staring at him with that dumb smile on your face," she clarified.

I let out a big belly laugh. "No, Gin is like my brother. I'm just happy for him. He has dreamed of playing in a tavern his whole life," I explained.

"That's sweet," she said. "What do ye want?"

"I want to travel and have adventurers," I said.

"A woman after me own heart," she said. "Once mam can find someone to work the tavern, I'm plannin' to get out of here."

"I wouldn't mind the company," I said. Was I flirting now? Is that what flirting feels like? I was always so focused on finding a way out that I never really explored any kind of a romantic relationship back home. Most people in my tribe stay together for life. Why lead someone on when I always planned on leaving?

"Ye wouldn't, would you? I wouldn't mind traveling with a big, strong woman like yeself. Ye're quite the looker, too," she complimented.

I was glad I wasn't drinking anything because I definitely would have spit it out. I did not expect this Gnome woman to find me attractive. I can't imagine she sees many Orcs in this small town.

"I'm Tilly," she offered.

"Karuk," I managed to get out.

"Well, Karuk, I hope you'll look me up before leavin' town. Maybe we can get to know each other a little better," she said with a wink. She walked away to find other customers.

I was relieved when I looked beside me and saw that Dara had left. It was a bit less embarrassing that no one I knew saw my first ever attempt at flirty banter.

Dara plopped back into the seat beside me. "I've found us a job!"

"Yeah? What are we doing?"

"Apparently, Old Man O'Reilly has been having some trouble with his beag sheep. He's been losing a couple every few days."

"Lost sheep? That doesn't exactly feel like an adventure," I complained.

"Begging adventurers can't be choosy adventurers," Dara said. "And who knows, maybe some sort of monster is eating them or something. There could be some action."

I relented and agreed to take the job. At least it was something.

Because we'd slept through the day, I wasn't really tired. Dara, Gin, and I ended up gathered around the table at the end of the night.

"It was amazing!" Gin beamed. "It was everything I'd ever dreamed of. They loved it, I loved it. I could do this forever!"

Dara patted him on the back. "That's great, Gin!"

"It was incredible to see other people into your music. You were definitely in your element," I observed.

"I really thought I was going to regret leaving in such a rush, but gods, this is the best!" Gin confessed.

The homesick feeling that had been nagging with me finally boiled over. I couldn't hold it in any longer. "I miss everyone," I blurted out.

Dara looked completely confused, like he didn't know what to do. Gin swiftly crawled across the table and jumped into my lap to give me a hug.

"It's o.k. Ruki! We're going to be heroes."

"I know. I'm glad we're doing it, but I can't believe I didn't tell anyone goodbye. I want to travel all over Galevyn, but The Jungle will always be my home." I used the fur shirt on Gin's shoulder to wipe my tears.

"We'll probably go back before you know it," Gin tried to reassure me.

I knew that his heart was in the right place, but my head wasn't hearing any of it. "But how long will that take? We barely even have money. We're gathering sheep tomorrow. We could be stuck here forever!"

"You can send a message," Dara said.

"What?" Gin and I said simultaneously.

"I'm a wizard, aren't I? I know a little bit of divination magic. We could send a message to your family."

"But I can't do magic. The shaman in my tribe tried to get me to do it when I was little and I was no good at it," I admitted.

"I can do all the hard parts, you just have to visualize the person you want to talk to and say the message," Dara explained.

I felt myself calming down a bit. "I think I can do that."

"See, Ruki! You're back before you know it, like I said. Well, your voice will be back, because of magic or something," Gin stumbled.

Dara explained that I was going to be the one to cast the spell ultimately, but he was going to write a scroll that could contain the spell. He pulled a blank scroll and his magic quill back out of his bag. He also pulled out a much smaller feather and a bottle of rosewater. He spent about ten minutes drawing an elaborate magic circle on the scrolls, featuring overlapping circles, triangles, and random scribbles I didn't recognize. He put the small feather in the center of the scroll, dipped his finger in the rose water, and traced the circle with the rosewater. He closed his eyes and grabbed the feather by its base with the tips of his fingers. He then yanked the feather out of the circle and it flashed a green light.

Dara opened his eyes and he was overcome with a wave of lethargy. "It's done."

"Are you o.k.?" Gin asked.

"Yeah, yeah," Dara reassured us. "Putting spells onto paper just takes a lot more out of me."

It meant a lot that he went through that for me. "Thank you."

"No problem. Honestly, it's nice to be able to do magic for people that appreciate it." Dara laughed. "All you've gotta do is place one hand on the scroll and the other hand on your head."

He demonstrated without actually touching the scroll.

"Then you just have to picture the person in your head and speak the message out loud. If they reply, you'll just hear it in your head. I'm going to go to bed now," Dara finished.

"You're the best, buddy!" Gin complimented.

Dara grinned at that. He's found his people.

I did as Dara instructed and I pictured my father in my head. I took a deep breath. "Dad? It's me, Karuk. I left The Jungle. I made a couple of friends and we're going to become adventurers. I know you don't understand. I don't expect you to. But I want you and mom to know I love you. I appreciate all you've done. I'll be home soon, once I become a hero."

It didn't take long for a reply to come. "Karuk? We were wondering where you were, but we weren't worried. We knew you could take care of yourself. Me and your mom knew this day would come. I'm glad you're making friends, you always had trouble doing that with the tribe. We love you. Take care of yourself."

I began to cry again, this time tears of joy. Gin had scooted a chair super close to mine while I was doing the ritual. He hugged me again.

"Did it work?" he asked.

"Yeah," I replied. "Yeah, it worked."

***

Dara, Gin, and I headed over to Old Man O'Reilly's field the following morning. He had a cozy farmhouse and a large, fenced pasture where the beag sheep grazed. I had never seen beag sheep before, but they were probably the cutest animals I have ever seen, and I'm not one to typically discuss the cuteness of animals. Beag sheep appeared to be like any other sheep, but were smaller and pastel-colored. That explained all of the pastel-colored clothing that most of the Gnomes wore.

Dara suggested we walk the perimeter of the fence for clues. The fence looked like it had been smashed in on one far end of the field, very far away from the farmhouse.

"Think this is our culprit?" Gin asked. "The sheep are just walking out and not coming back?"

I walked up to the broken wood.

"This looks like it's been smashed. Maybe there is a monster involved." I really didn't know much about what sort of monsters lived in Ronan, but I had images of a manticore; a lion with Dragon's wings and a scorpion tail. Or a chimera, a creature with three heads, one each of a lion, goat, and Dragon, and its tail is a snake. Those were two of my favorites from the songs. I didn't dare dream I might get to fight a Dragon, like Tadarin, or drake, which is like a smaller dragon.

Dara walked up to join me and closely examined the broken fence.

"I don't think it's a monster," Dara began.

"Dammit," I said.

He crouched down and touched the broken ends of the fence. "But we may still end up fighting something. These cuts are clean. Someone cut this fence to look like it had been smashed. Someone is framing a monster. We've got ourselves a livestock thief on our hands."

"Woohoo! This is getting interesting!" Gin exclaimed.

After Dara discovered that a person had abducted the beag sheep, our next steps seemed pretty obvious.

"So, we just want to follow whatever trail there is to find the missing sheep?" I asked.

"I don't think there's a trail, Karuk," Dara observed.

"Yeah, this break in the fence is the only thing here," Gin agreed.

It was almost cute how little they both knew about tracking. I grew up in a hunting tribe in the jungles of Anglachel. I don't care who took these sheep, there was some sort of trail.

"I can track them."

"Are we sure we just want to go straight to the sheep? Don't we want to figure out who took the sheep?" Dara questioned. "When we thought it was a monster, the motive was sustenance. But why would someone try to make it look like a monster took them?"

"You're thinking about this too much," I complained.

"He might have a point, Ruki," Gin joined in. "This person's motive might tell us how dangerous they are. Maybe we don't have to go climbing all over the hills of Ronan if this person is still in town."

I decided to humor him. "Let's pretend like that's the best idea. Where would we even start?"

"We'd have to investigate," Dara began. "We would need to talk to people in town and see if there is anyone that had ever expressed any ill will towards Old Man O'Reilly."

"That sounds dumb. We're just going to follow the trail," I decided. I walked through the hole in the fence and began looking for clues. I wasn't sure if they were going to follow me, but after my abrupt dive off the boat, they knew that if I thought I had the best path forward, I wasn't going to be stopped. I heard voices in the background, but I blocked them out because I was already in tracking mode.

Whoever had taken these sheep was pretty good at covering their trail. There really wasn't much left. But they weren't good enough to fool me. While this person was obviously treading lightly and trying not to leave any evidence, sheep are going to do what sheep are going to do. The most obvious sign of movement was the subtle trail left by the beag sheep in the grass. Admittedly, it was reassuring that the sheep were walking themselves. They could still be alive if this person hadn't decided to kill them right away or load them up in some sort of vehicle. It also meant they probably weren't very far away. As I continued following the trail, I could hear footsteps behind me. I was glad Gin and Dara had come to their senses.

The hoof tracks led us to a rockier set of hills near the beach. The trail became slightly harder to follow, because the sheep wouldn't leave much of an indention in stone, but it looked like our culprit had traveled this way many times. There were signs of well-worn hand and foot holes along the hillside. This person had been climbing to avoid leaving much of a foot trail. That was smart. Most people wouldn't look along the steeper parts of the hill for clues.

"Are we going to be there soon?" Gin whined.

"I don't know, Gin. I didn't make this trail," I reminded him.

Gin sighed. "I know, but did they leave any sign that they're close to where they brought the sheep? My sandals were not made to climb rocky hills like this."

"What do you expect? A note that says, 'stolen sheep pen just ahead?'" I sarcastically asked.

"Probably not?" Gin said skeptically. "Or did they? Is this a trick to embarrass me?"

"You can't be serious." I laughed. "No, Gin, they didn't leave a note or any other sign that we're getting close. This person is actually pretty good. They've been trying to hide their tracks."

"Should we be worried?" Dara asked.

"I don't think so. So far, all the signs I've seen belong to one person and a small group of sheep. I think this person is working alone."

"That's reassuring," Dara said. "I don't know if we could fight a bunch of people."

"Don't worry, I'll protect both of you. No matter what we run into, I've got you," I said.

Dara's face relaxed in relief. "I'm glad."

We continued up the rocky hill for about thirty more minutes. We had to double back a couple of times because they had left false trails. Eventually, we ended up at the opening of a cave. We also began to hear bleating sounds.

"Is that the sheep? That sounds like the sheep," Gin inquired.

"I think so, but we don't know what sort of stuff we're going to encounter in there. Both of you stay behind me," I instructed them.

We eased into the cave and it was very dark. My Orcish heritage allowed me to see in pretty dark areas, but I couldn't see much in the way of details. With that being said, I did spot a pile of way too extravagant pillows for a cave along the right wall. I drew my hand ax just in case we ran into any trouble. I began to approach it. I saw something squirming and a tiny pair of wings.

"What is that?" I thought aloud.

Before I could stop him, Dara walked past me to approach the pillows.

"I think that's a . . . Ah!" he exclaimed. Gin and I also yelped a bit.

Dara had triggered a net trap. As we began to be suspended in the air, I lost my grip and my ax clattered to the ground below. A rope net tightened around us and we all became much closer than we had been the previous night in the single room.

"Baby gwiber," Dara finished. "I think that's a baby gwiber. It is a snake with wings. I don't remember reading about them being native to Ronan. That little guy is pretty far from home."

"Fascinatin'," Gin flatly commented. "Do you think you could get your elbow out of my crotch?"

Dara frantically and apologetically readjusted himself, which only made the whole situation more uncomfortable for the rest of us. The net began swinging dangerously.

"Could we stop moving?" I asked in a way that sounded more like a command. "None of us like this. We have to figure a way out. Dara, could you burn us out?"

"I don't think so," Dara observed. "This is a little too tight for me to cast my spells. I have to gesture and I can't really do that here."

"O.K. Gin, can you play your drum to conjure a barrier to cut us out?"

"You really think I can beat on a drum with your ass shoved up against it?" he grumbled.

Then it was up to me. I began staring at the rope to see if there was a weak spot I could push to break it. This all would have been easier if I hadn't dropped my hand ax. This was a mess of a first adventure.

"What're you lot doing here?" A female voice called from the mouth of the cave. I looked over and saw a bundle of curls atop a backlit short silhouette. I recognized the voice.

"Tilly?" I questioned the figure.

"And of course you recognize me. I didn't want to kill you. I was hoping I could clear this place out before you placed me. Oh well," she conceded, drawing a dagger from her side that shone in the sunlight.

"Kill us?" Gin worriedly screamed.

Tilly chucked a dagger in our direction and I managed to jump a bit, causing the net to bounce up as the dagger swung in our direction. I timed it just right so it would slice through one of the bottom ropes. As the net swung back down, I pushed myself feet first through the newly formed hole. I landed and scooped my hand ax up in a single motion.

"You're not killing anybody today," I replied, taking a defensive position.

"That was all very cool, Ruki," Gin said. "But do you think you could help us down? Not all of us are as athletic as you and it is taking everything I've got to hold onto these ropes."

I looked up and saw Dara and Gin clinging to the rope net so they wouldn't crash into the cave floor beneath. But I couldn't focus on them right now.

"Hang on a bit longer," I advised and rushed up to Tilly.

"Whoa, whoa, whoa," Dara shouted across the cave. "Nobody has to kill anyone. Tilly, was it? Why do you think you have to kill us?"

"Ye're adventurers, aren't ye?" she said. "You're going to want to kill my baby over there. That's what adventurers do, right? KIll rare creatures?"

"You must have heard some nasty rumors," Gin reassured. "Or we don't know as much about adventuring as we thought. We don't want to kill anything unless we have to."

"Truly?" Tilly asked.

"Yes," I shouted, trying to tamp down the adrenaline coursing through my veins. Tilly lowered her dagger.

I used the moment to help Gin and Dara down from the net. Then if she decided to turn on us again, at least we'd all be able to fight. Once we dusted off our clothes and took a moment to stretch a bit, Dara began to walk towards her slowly.

"What is a baby gwiber doing here?" he asked. "I thought they were native to Daragon."

"I don't know, I just found her one day. A big egg washed up on the beach and wings hatched out of it. I've been takin' care of her ever since. I didn't tell anybody because I know how my community reacts to anything weird or dangerous," Tilly explained.

"That's why you needed the beag sheep," Dara concluded.

"Yeah, she needed more meat than I could swipe from the kitchen at the Ale and Cabbage. Stealing sheep seemed like my best option."

"We can help you get her somewhere safe," Dara said.

"Really? Where? Do you want to take her to Daragon?" Tilly asked.

"We don't need to go that far," he explained. "I've know about a magical creature reserve across the mountains in Reyes."

"Would all of you really want to help me after I tried to kill you? Well, at least strongly considered it."

"Do you promise not to try to kill us again?" Gin asked.

Tilly paused like she was thinking about it. "Sure."

Gin chuckled at the bit. "Then we're good."

I wasn't so sure, but I felt confident that I could watch our backs around her and keep us safe, now that I had some sense of what she could do.

"If the two of you are good with it, I'll let her come," I said.

"We should probably just leave," Tilly said. "I don't want to explain this to my mam."

"No," I remembered how much I missed my tribe when I left without saying goodbye. "We're going back and you're going to explain it to her. I'll go with you, but you're going to tell her."

"And I left my backup components in my room there anyway," Dara said.

"Ruki," Gin said.

"Yeah," I replied, looking down at him.

"Saving a magical creature and traveling across a continent feels like a proper adventure," he said.

"That it does," I agreed. I reached down and put my hand on his shoulder. He placed his hand on mine. And that's the story of how Gin and I became adventurers.

Chapter Five

I'm Sure It's Fine

WE HEADED BACK TO the Cabbage and Ale to speak with Tilly's grandmother. Once we explained to her that Tilly had found a baby flying snake called a gwiber and that we needed to take it to a magical creature reserve to keep it safe, she was surprisingly accommodating.

"I knew this day would come," she said, nodding while her graying reddish curls gently bounced on her head.

Tilly cocked her head in confusion. "Mam, you always talked to me about how I would take over the Cabbage and Ale one day. Why would you do that if you knew I was going to leave?"

"You will learn one day. It is a grandmother's job to make their grandchild feel guilty about leaving. I just

wanted to make sure you knew what ye were leavin',"
she said.

She helped Tilly pack and even gave us a map to help
us cross the mountains. Gin, Dara, and I stood outside
the tavern while Tilly finished her goodbyes. Watching
her hug her grandma warmed my heart. I was glad we
could make sure Tilly's grandma got more than I left
my family. Tilly bounded in our direction, cradling the
gwiber.

"Are we doin' this?" she asked.

"You betcha!" Gin exclaimed. "Do we just hike up
the mountains like we did when we tracked your cave?"

"According to this map, we have two options," Dara
began. "We can try to find a passageway under the
mountains, or climb over them."

"Under sounds easier," I offered.

"It does," Dara agreed. "But my Dwarvish isn't the
best. I don't know if I could talk our way in."

"I know a bit," Tilly said. "Every now and then, the
Dwarves come to the Cabbage and Ale between expe-
ditions. They're pretty into my grandma's cookin'."

"That sounds promising!" Gin yelled.

"Sure, between the two of us, we should be able to
figure something out," Dara agreed.

We followed the dirt road out of town and stopped
at the base of the mountains, where the road just sort of
abruptly ended. Tilly told us that some of the traders

use goats to cross the mountains, but they just pack everything on the goats and ride straight up the cliffside.

"The map says the entrance to the Dwarven part of Ferreria is to the north of this road," Dara explained. "It looks like the door should be marked with a symbol of a triangular science beaker."

"What's a science beaker?" Gin asked, and I was glad because I had the same question. We studied nature and learned new things in The Jungle, but we didn't use science in the way Anglachellean society thinks of it. Mercifully, Dara just showed us the picture instead of trying to explain all of the science to us.

"Why would they use a beaker for their symbol? Everything I have ever read about Dwarves referred to them as miners," Dara inquired.

"That's actually a nasty stereotype," Tilly stated. "They do mine. Most of the dwarves that swung by the C&A did a lot of mining, but they did it to study the rocks. It's not about gettin' it, it's about studying it."

Dara's face lit up at learning something new. "Fascinating."

We walked up and down the edge of the mountain range, closely inspecting every odd-looking group of rock formations. If there were doors there, they were awfully well hidden.

Finally, Tilly started peering down an opening between two different outcroppings of rocks.

"I think I got somethin'!" She had since handed the gwiber-sitting duty off to Gin, who was having an absolute blast trying to teach the flying snake to flap its wings to the beat of his drum. Tilly used her small Gnomish frame to climb through a small opening in the rocks and was standing inside a tiny overhang.

"I don't think this is right, Tilly," I said. I still didn't fully trust this girl, and her instincts certainly weren't going to be what I trusted first. "Aren't Dwarves a lot stouter than you? They wouldn't be able to squeeze in there as you did."

"Of course not," Tilly shrugged off. "They must have some science-y doohickey that opens it for 'em."

I approached the outcropping and started inspecting the rock cage that Tilly was now standing inside. They looked like normal rocks. There didn't appear to be a seam or anything that showed a place the rocks would move into to open it up for a Dwarf-sized user. But Tilly was convinced; I could see in the columns of light peeking through the rocks' openings that she was fiddling with something inside.

"I'm coming inside," I announced.

"How? You can't fit!" Tilly complained.

"I'll just bust through the rocks. I can't let you be in there by yourself. You might get hurt," I said, trying to explain why I needed to keep watch on her.

"Or you think I'll leave you three behind," Tilly said, accurately accusing me. "Don't forget, your Goblin friend has the gwiber. I wouldn't leave him behind."

She was right, but I still wanted in there to ensure she wasn't making us wait around while she poked at some random rocks before realizing it wasn't an entrance to Ferreria. I pulled my hand ax out of its sheath and started tapping away at the rocks at the top of the entrance.

"Watch it, Orc girl! You might trigger somethin'," Tilly whined.

"I'm sure it's fine," I assured her.

I successfully chipped one rock column away when I felt the ground shake under my feet. I could tell by the unchanging expressions of Gin and Dara that it was only just happening where Tilly and I were standing.

Tilly looked smug, she seemed to be enjoying this. "I told you."

Abruptly, the ground beneath Tilly and I slid away. We fell into the darkness below.

The fall happened fast. Usually, time kind of slows down when you have a dramatic fall, but when you're falling in complete darkness, I guess your brain can't really process what's happening. As we were falling, I needed to position Tilly on top of me. I knew that my Orcish frame could handle the fall much better than her tiny Gnomish one.

"What are you doin?!" Tilly yelled at me when I put my hand on her to usher her in my direction.

"Trying to save your life!' I screamed back, continuing to pull her.

"Who said I need saving?!"

"No one needed to say it! We're falling down a dark pit, I have no idea what's at the bottom. Your little body won't be able to take the fall the way I can."

"I can see down there, it looks like just flat stone," she said as I smashed into it. It definitely stung, but I'd spread my body out enough to even out the impact across it. Tilly scrambled off of me as my eyes began to adjust to the darkness. She began examining the wall.

"Are you guys o.k.?" Gin's voice emanated from the hole at the top.

"I'll live," I responded.

"Do you see a way out? Maybe a button or an emergency ladder?" Dara asked.

"No, it looks like a sheer rock wall the whole way," Tilly shouted up.

"We'll figure something out," Dara said, less reassuringly than I'm sure he intended. "Maybe I can figure something out with Gin's barrier magic."

"Sounds good," I said. "I could use a few minutes to rest."

Tilly turned in my direction and rushed to my leg. My head followed her, and I could see what had worried her. My leg was covered in blood. I felt pain there, but it wasn't any worse than the pain running through the rest of my body from the fall.

"Karuk! You have to let me patch you up!" she said urgently.

"Go ahead," I relented. "I"m not exactly in a position to stop you."

Tilly pulled out a candle and lit it. She lifted my leg and examined it all over.

"It looks like it's just a really bad scrape. You should be fine, but I need to clean you up and cover it, so it doesn't get infected."

"How do you know first aid?"

"I was always an accident-prone child, and my grandma taught me what she was doing every time she took care of me."

"I never needed to know that kind of thing. My tribe doesn't let us travel alone if they can help; we always have a healer with each group. That allowed people like me to focus on hunting," I said.

"I get that," she said. "But if we're going to be traveling together, you really should learn a bit of first aid yourself. Someone needs to be able to put me back together if I go down."

"I wouldn't let any of you get hurt," I said, a bit surprised that I'd actually meant it.

"And how is that working out for you?" Tilly asked as she pulled a flask out of her belt and twisted the cap off it. She poured the brown liquid on my open wound.

"Ahhhh!" I wailed.

"That's what I thought." This girl loved being right.

"Hey, that's cheating!" I retorted.

"There is no cheating in love and war." She laughed.

"And which one is this?" I asked. "We weren't really fighting anyone when we fell."

"Working with you feels like a bit of both," Tilly said thoughtfully.

"I'm not always like this," I said apologetically. "I just don't trust easily. It is hard to forget you trapping us in that net and talking about killing us."

"You don't need to apologize," Tilly said. "I get it; I'd feel the same way. And honestly, I don't want you to change around me. I kind of like feeling the thrill of worrying that you're either going to punch me or kiss me."

"That doesn't sound healthy," I jested. "I'd only punch you if you deserved it."

"Don't you kink-shame me!" Tilly joked back. "I'm just tryin' to tell you that I like you the way you are."

That did something to me. I never felt like I fit in with my tribe. They were all about preserving the jungle, and they would never have understood how much I wanted to see the world. I knew Gin cared about me, but I always worried he was just putting up with me because we were the only ones that understood each other. Tilly telling me she liked me the way I am was something new. I felt something warm on my cheeks.

"Thank you," I managed to get out.

"Don't mention it. Don't go getting mushy on me, we've got a lot of land to travel before we deliver the gwiber."

"Right," I replied.

The room began to brighten as a pink spiral staircase began crawling down the walls of the hole.

"Is that you, Gin?" I yelled up.

"He can't really talk," Dara shouted back down. "He has to concentrate and play really softly."

"He must hate that," I yelled back up.

"Shut up, Ruki!" Gin screamed quickly.

The pink staircase stuttered out of existence for a second.

"Maybe don't bother him right now," Tilly suggested.

"Yeah, you're probably right," I said, chuckling.

"Race you up the stairs?" Tilly challenged.

"You're on," I said, rushing in front of her to be the first to start climbing.

Chapter Six

Passing Through Montläken

It took us a while, but we eventually found an entrance into the Dwarven settlements under the mountains. After we found the trapped door, identifying another set of rocks that were a bit off-color from the rest of the mountain was just a matter of finding it. I let Tilly do her thing this time, and she was able to get us in. The first set of Dwarf guards we ran into were hesitant about letting us in, but Gin was able to talk them into it. Part of me thinks the novelty of seeing an Orc and a Goblin was enough to get us through.

Before long, we found ourselves in the massive Dwarven city of Montläken. The city was completely under the mountain, but you wouldn't know it from where we were standing. The stone around the city had been carved into a smooth dome that extended into the air for what looked like nearly 3,000 squares. Standing at the entrance, I could have thought I was looking at Anglachel were it not for the tunnels that dotted the streets. There was an earthy smell that filled the air.

"What do you think those are?" I asked Dara, gesturing to one of the tunnels.

"They must be mining tunnels. It is simply fascinating that they treat these tunnels the way we treat any other kind of infrastructure in Anglachel," Dara beamed.

It made sense. The sound of explosions, likely creating new mines, were nearly constant.

"It's where they all work, it's got to be part of the city," Tilly reasoned.

"So what do we do now?" Gin asked. "Just walk through the city and find a way out on the other side?"

Dara shrugged. "That's as good a suggestion as anything I could come up with."

We entered the city limits, and Montläken only grew more impressive. The buildings appeared to be carved out of the same stone as the ground. They'd literally carved their buildings out of the mountain instead of constructing them. I couldn't even begin to fathom the amount of forethought that planning this city would have taken. This would have been enough to blow my mind fully, but then I noticed the fine detail carved into each building. They'd carved all of this by hand! I would have been willing to bet they'd used magic to dig out this place.

We had only begun admiring the city whenever we were stopped by the local guards.

"Grüezi," one of the guards said, speaking in Dwarven.

Tilly uttered a couple of things back and forth with him until she eventually turned to us and said, "They said they'll take us to the King. They said he'll probably want to meet us anyway, and he can speak North Elven like you."

"Should that worry us?" I asked. I didn't know much about Dwarven culture, but I did know that being escorted to the leader of a nation immediately after entering didn't seem like the most normal thing to happen.

"Nah," Tilly replied. "In my experience, Dwarves work hard, but they're mostly friendly. Brusque but friendly."

I wasn't entirely convinced, but I was trying to start trusting Tilly. I kept my apprehension to myself and followed. We were led around a large, central lake to a towering castle with pyramid-shaped roofs topping the different towers. It also appeared to be carved directly out of the mountain. Flags were flying on the rooftops.

They showed the same image of the science beaker Dara had shown us before we entered. I guess doing science really is what they prioritize.

We were led through a long hallway until we finally made it to a huge set of doors.

"King in there," one of the guards said in broken North Elven.

I looked around, and my party looked pretty apprehensive. They were definitely feeling the same way as me. I knew one of us had to be brave, and since I'd already shoved my doubts into the back of my mind, it was up to me. I walked up to the door and pushed it open. I could feel my friends following at my heels. The throne room was modest in comparison to the rest of the city. It was large enough to hold twenty or so people at most. Directly in front of us was a set of five steps that led to the throne. The steps and the throne were connected with the floor. There was an intimidating Dwarven figure sitting on it. He sat stoically, so I continued to walk forward.

I didn't know enough about Dwarven culture to know who this person was. Obviously, he was a king since the guards said so, but was he the king of the entire Dwarven nation of Ferreira? Or was he just the king of Montläken? Did Dwarves even consider themselves part of one nation? I was starting to wonder why we even agreed to come here.

"Do my eyes deceive me, or do I see an Orc, a human, a Gnome, and a Goblin? What a curious party to pass through Montläken," the king said with a bright yet gravelly voice. His face was covered with a bushy beard, but the top of it seemed to rise, indicating he was smiling.

"Yes, sir," I began. "We were hoping to pass through Montläken in order to reach Reyes."

"Would it be safe to presume you are a group of adventurers then?" the king asked.

"Yes! We definitely are!" Gin said excitedly. "What gave it away? Is it because we look so cool and strong?"

"Something like that," the king said, a slight giggle in his voice. This was going better than I thought. He at least seemed happy to see us. "I will grant you passage," he stated. "But I need you to do something for me in return."

"Anything," Tilly immediately responded.

"The tunnels we use to mine obsidian have been challenging to access for the past month. It has greatly set us back on our research," the king explained.

"So you need us to do the research?" Dara asked hopefully.

"I'm sure you are smart," the king said. "But I was hoping you could provide a more violent solution."

"We can do violent!" Gin exclaimed. "Ruki here is an incredible fighter!"

"Good, good. The tunnel has been infested with imps. You see, if we dig deep enough, our tunnels tap into The Hells. Nasty things sometimes find their way in. Our researchers aren't equipped for combat, and our guards are really mostly for ceremonial purposes. You would be doing us a great favor if you could clear out the imps. If you could find a way to stop them from entering, that would be even better. Follow the tunnel, it will eventually lead you to the city of Valnan. Valnan will have an entrance to Reyes. Bring back something unique from the tunnel that we haven't studied yet, and I'm certain the King of Valnan will reward you handsomely."

"Awesome!" Gin said. "We're in!"

*****

The imps infesting the Dwarve's obsidian tunnel were actually pretty easy to take out. They were essentially bats with tiny humanoid bodies and heads. As far as I could tell, they weren't sentient, just wild animals. The tunnel itself was well lit with glass tubes affixed to either side. The glass tubes shined with a dull orange light, similar to candlelight but more consistent. Occasionally, the tunnel got dark because the imps had smashed up the magic lights. Dara was able to quickly conjure a bit of light that we could fight by. I know that we had figured out what was happening to Old Man O'Reilly's beag sheep and we are currently helping Tilly get her baby gwiber to Daragon, but slaying these things felt like our first real adventure. Striking down demonic vermin was the kind of thing me and Gin would talk about doing.

Eventually, we came to a fork in the tunnel. The magic lights had been busted up on both sides of the fork and it wasn't clear which was the right way to go. There was broken glass on either side.

"Which way?" Gin asked the group.

Dara started rummaging in his bag. "Gimme a sec, I'm going to see what I can find out."

He pulled out a crystal and tightened his fist around it. He closed his eyes and reached out his hand, moving it around like a dowsing rod. He did this for a couple of minutes until his eyes snapped back open and he faced us again.

"It's weird," he began. "Both sides show powerful magic."

"Maybe both ways lead to Valnan," Tilly suggested. "It is the next city along this path."

Dara pursed his lips in thought. "I don't think so."

"What is it?" I asked.

"It's just. . . this side feels like identification and transmutation magic," he said, pointing down the right path. "This way feels like destruction and elemental magic."

"You're the only one here that has any idea what any of this means, buddy," Gin urged him. "Why don't you just tell us what you're thinking."

"The Dwarves worship the goddess Lovelace. She rules over identification and destruction magic," Dara explained.

"Identification sounds more like Dwarves," Tilly suggested. "They're all about research and stuff."

"That's my first instinct too. But they could be using destruction to carve out new tunnels. It really could be either side."

"What do we have to worry about if we get it wrong?" I asked him.

"Well, these imps have to be coming from some-where. I've never read anything that says where The Hells are, but it makes as much sense as anything else that they could be way underground," Dara reasoned.

"So we either make it to the city or we go to hell?" Gin asked.

"Pretty much," Dara confirmed.

I put my hand on his shoulder. "Do we want to reason this or do you just want to decide? We trust you either way."

"Elemental sounds like demons and devils, ya' know, fire and stuff," Dara said. "But we know for sure that the Dwarves use elemental magic, that's what all these lights have been conjured from. And it frankly feels more like them to use destruction magic to build with than transmutation. They carved that whole dome and their buildings from the same stone and the extra had to go somewhere, unless it didn't. Destruction magic fully destroys the matter it is used on and converts it to magical energy. To me, that makes more sense than them using transmutation magic. It would just turn the stone into something else."

"So head towards destruction?" Gin asked.

Dara was having trouble trusting himself. His eyes were darting back and forth. "I think so."

I still didn't like not being sure. I knew what I had to do. "O.K., just wait here, guys. I'll sneak ahead since I can see in the dark."

"Hold on, Karuk!" Tilly interjected. "I can see in the dark, too. I'm coming with you."

My mouth instinctively lifted into a grin. I looked to the ground to hide it. "O.K."

We crept into the darkness, walking silently for about five minutes. After Tilly admitted she liked me in the hole trap, I felt awkward whenever it was just the two of us.

"So Dara is pretty impressive," Tilly whispered, just loud enough that I could hear her, but no more.

I was a little worried that my voice wouldn't get that soft and I'd give us away. "Yeah, it seems like he can do pretty much anything with magic."

"I was pretty sure that people could only ever do one discipline of magic at a time, but he's done both divination and elemental just in this tunnel."

I knew a little bit about magic, but not enough to keep a conversation going. We walked in silence for a bit longer. I should say something. I looked around for something to talk about."This mine tunnel is really smooth."Gods, why did I say that? Who cares about the the roughness or smoothness of rock?

"Yeah, it must be destruction magic, like Dara said. It's weird, right?" she responded.

Whew, she thought it was interesting. What now? Should I compliment her?"Your hair is curly."

"Yes, Karuk. Are we just saying things we see now?"

Dammit. How did I think that was a compliment? I spotted wings flapping towards us in the distance."Imp ahead," I warned.

Tilly drew her dagger and took a fighting position. I drew my ax. The flapping got close enough that we could hear it. I charged towards the imp. I was running faster than I had before and I lost my footing, tumbling to the ground.

"Karuk!" Tilly yelled, as she rushed towards me and the imp. She jumped and used the wall for leverage to jump again. The dagger slashed through the imp and two wings clattered to the ground. I could now see that what we thought was an imp was actually a bat. I rolled over and laughed.

"What?" Tilly looked offended. "Did I do something weird? Was my form off?"

"No," I managed between laughs. "We were scared of a bat!"

"Oh my gods, really?" Tilly asked. She picked up one of the wings and joined in my laughter. "Sorry, pal." She fell down on top of me. Her small body felt warm in the cool mine air.

"Me too," I said.

"You too what?" Tilly asked.

"I like you, too."

***

We rejoined Gin and Dara and after a very long walk in near darkness, we began to see light at the end of the tunnel. It was a bright, white light, similar to what it looked like when we left Montläken. There were a pair of Dwarven guards standing on the other side of the well-lit hole.

"What are you doing there?" a gruff feminine voice asked. Their armor made them indistinguishable. It seemed like, at least among the guards, Dwarves didn't care about gender. I appreciated that.

"We've been sent here on a mission from the King of Montläken!" Gin exclaimed.

"Are you telling me you four took care of the imps in this tunnel?" the other guard asked.

"You know it! Don't you ever forget that the Misfits of Fortune did that for you!" Gin said.

"What did you just call us?" I asked.

Gin puffed his chest out. He had clearly considered this moment. "Our name. The Misfits of Fortune! It sounds like something that would be sung about, right?"

"I mean, sure," I said. "We can workshop it later." I turned my attention back to the guards. "The King of Montläken said we should talk to your King."

"Oh yes, I'm sure he'll want to reward you," the Dwarven woman said.

"Shit!" Tilly cursed.

"What is it?" I asked.

"I forgot about finding something rare," she explained.

"Is this anything?" Gin said, holding up a hard gemstone, colored in a swirl pattern of amber and obsidian.

Dara's eyes widened. "Gin! That's concentrated transmutation magic!"

"So, it's something?" he asked hopefully.

"It's really rare. It is definitely something," Dara said.

"Yay! We did it!" Gin shouted in celebration.

Chapter Seven

Just Get Over Here

After weeks of travel under the mountains, through Dwarven and Devil territory, we'd finally made it to Reyes. The exit out of Valnan opened into a narrow rockface along the ocean. We had to carefully skirt across it until we'd reached the broader side of the mountain. The Dwarves of Ferrerira really knew how to hide their settlements. The mountain was covered in grass and opened into a large field. It was wild to think that less than a month ago, I'd never traveled beyond Anglachel. Gin and I were really, truly adventurers.

There weren't any obvious roads, but Dara was able to send another message using divination magic to one of his former classmates from Arcana University who was finishing up his practicum at the magical creature reserve we were headed towards. He instructed Dara to wait next to the mountain, and he would come to pick us up.

"What do you think he'll pick us up with?" Gin excitedly asked. "Maybe a Dragon with a broken wing? Or a herd of alaricorns? Oh, Oh! What if it's a panther!"

"Don't even joke about that," Dara snapped.

"What? I don't know anything about panthers. Are they scary or something?" Gin asked.

"Your tribe must have similar stories to mine," I said. As far as I knew, no one had actually seen a panther. At least, no one had seen one and lived to talk about it. They were the sort of things the older folks would scare kids with. "If you don't eat your vegetables, the panther will come to get you!" That sort of thing.

"Sure, I've heard the stories," Gin answered. "But we're adventures now! Don't you want to see one for yourself? They might not be so scary."

"All I ever learned about panthers at Arcana University is that you don't want to run into one. The textbooks describe them as 'cat-like,' but that's all it ever says. I would like to see one, but there is no way we're ready to fight one yet," Dara explained.

Tilly threw her arm around Gin's shoulders. "Let the little guy have his fun. It's not like you say the word 'panther' and one appears."

"You're right," Dara said apologetically. "Sorry I snapped at you, Gin."

"You're good, buddy. You're probably right. We'll see a panther one day, but we probably shouldn't see one today," Gin agreed.

Before we could move on to another topic, we saw something bounding toward us from across the field.

Dara pointed to the figure in the distance. "This is probably him now."

The approaching mass looked small at first, but as it got closer, we could tell this was a massive creature. It looked sort of similar to a boar, but it had a much larger nose and different coloring. The creature had white stripes along its side, like a skunk, but with many more stripes. It galloped in our direction like a horse. A Human man rode atop it.

"Dara! Don't tell me you made friends!" the man yelled in our direction.

"Reggie! How are you?" Dara tried shouting over the pounding hooves.

The large creature came to a stop about two squares away from us. Reggie tossed one leg over the animal and slid down its flank. He tossed a feather in the air before he landed and it slowed his descent. As he landed, he walked in our direction.

"Sorry, I didn't catch that," Reggie said. He had tan skin and dark, tousled hair. The kind of hair that looked intentionally messy, but would probably take all morning to get to look that way. The mud on his work pants and thick button-up shirt indicated that it actually just fell that way naturally on his head. It was infuriating.

"I said that it's been forever, Reggie! How are you?" Dara said, offering his hand to Reggie. He took it and pulled Dara into a deep hug.

"I'm doing great, buddy. I'm loving it out here. But it is great to see a familiar face. There's no one around here that looks like me," he confided.

"That must be hard," Gin said facetiously since we'd been the only Orc and Goblin around ever since we'd started our journey. Reggie didn't seem to get it.

"It really has," Reggie agreed. "But I can't believe that little Dara has made a friend, much less three of them. Are you doing an adventuring practicum?"

"Something like that," Dara said, lowering his head to look at the ground.

"No, we are adventurers!" Gin interjected. "We just fought some imps under these mountains!"

Reggie let out a long whistle. "Traveling through the Hells. Dean Constance must have it out for you."

"Yeah," Dara said, looking off into the distance. He started scratching the back of his neck.

"So what is this thing?" Tilly said, mercifully changing the subject.

Reggie gestured towards the boar creature. "Oh, this little feller? This is a Giant Tapir. This one's just a baby, you can tell from the stripes along its side. The adults have solid-colored flanks."

"That's a baby? It is enormous! How big are the adults?" I said, trying to keep us on this topic a bit longer. I was also genuinely curious. This "baby" was as tall as a large tree in the jungle.

"This guy's about finished growing. He's just not lost his stripes. We took him in because we found him about a mile outside of the reserve without a mama. We presumed poachers hunted her. They get some good money from their pelts," Reggie said. He was clearly in his element talking about these creatures. "You said in your message you had something for me?"

"Yea," Tilly answered. She took the backpack-bed we'd fashioned to keep the gwiber in. The winged snake began to stir and poked its head out of the bag.

"Oh my goodness," Reggie exclaimed. "What a cutie!"

"I found her just outside of my village. I'm from Éindí Grá," Tilly elaborated.

"What would a gwiber be doing in Ronan? They usually aren't found outside of Daragon," Reggie asked himself.

"We were hoping you might be able to tell us," Dara said. "Or at least be able to take her off our hands."

"Yeah, sure," Reggie agreed. "I'm sure my boss would love to have one of these in the reserve. Arcana University provides funding for each magical creature we house."

"And she'll be safe?" Tilly asked.

"Couldn't be safer," Reggie assured her. "If there's anywhere that will make sure she grows up happy, it's here."

I visibly saw Tilly take a sigh of relief.

"Shall we?" Reggie offered, gesturing towards the Giant Tabir.

"Definitely!" Gin cried out.

Once we got to the animal reserve, Dara had to go make arrangements with Reggie and his boss. Gin offered to take care of the gwiber until they returned. I think he'd grown attached to the little thing. That left me and Tilly waiting by ourselves on the edge of the reserve. We sat on a fence surrounding a herd of Beag Sheep. It was interesting that we were ending our time together around the animals that first brought us together.

Tilly looked out at the rising and falling mountains in the distance. They were covered in green, with the occasional brown spot, where the mountain shifted into rock. The closest had a waterfall running down it. "It's beautiful here,"

"Yeah," I agreed. "Are you going to be o.k. making it back home? Do you want us to go with you?"

"You worried about me, big girl?" Tilly teased.

"We came this far together. It seems wrong to leave you behind."

"I agree. It seems a shame to leave us behind," Tilly replied.

"You have become one of us. The team could use someone like you if you'd want to stick around," I said. I lifted my arm to brush my hair out of my face, but really I was covering up the crimson that was surely spreading across my cheeks.

"Really, Karuk? The team wants me to stick around?" Tilly laughed. "You're going to have to do me one better than that."

"I wouldn't mind if you stuck around either." I turned my head, finally looking down at her. She had been staring at me, and our eyes met.

"Why don't you just say that you like me? Do you want me to say it? I like you, Karuk. I want to travel with you to see if this is anything."

I felt something in my stomach I'd never felt before. Like a flock of birds were flapping away down there. I squatted down to make our faces even.

"Do you care if I—" "I began.

"Just get over here," Tilly interrupted, pulling my face to hers. Her lips were soft but demanding. She kept pulling me in for more. Her hand ran through my hair, and I placed my hand on her back and pulled her deeper into the kiss. I didn't know how much time passed. It could have been minutes, it could have been an hour. Finally, we pulled apart and looked each other in the eyes again.

"That'll do, Ruki," Tilly said, smirking.

"I told you only Gin gets to call me that," I chided.

"We'll see. I want to check on my girl before we leave her behind. Race you to Gin?" Tilly asked.

"As if you even had to ask," I said, sprinting past her.

"That's cheating, Ruki!" she said, chasing after me.

Chapter Eight

The Magic Animal Reserve

Gin

THIS PLACE IS INCREDIBLE! I have spent my life in the jungle feeling like I'd seen every plant and animal there was to see, but here I am surrounded by hundreds I'd never even heard of. I mean, I'd never even heard of a gwiber, and now I've been traveling with Gintina for weeks now. I've named the gwiber Gintina, by the way. She kept looking at me with her cute beady eyes like she wanted a name so I decided to give her one.

Dara went to talk with Reggie about making arrangements for Gintina's new home and Ruki and Tilly ran off together. They're probably going to kiss or something. I think it's been obvious to everyone but Ruki that they're in love. I hope Tilly finally tells her. I've been dying to tease her about it ever since we met Tilly, but I knew it'd be more romantic if she figured it out on her own. I'm a sucker for good romance, it always makes a great story.

I figured while everyone else was busy, Gintina and I should look around this place. If it was going to be her new home, she was going to have to meet her new roommates. Our first stop was a large green space surrounded by a fence. A beautiful white horse walked up to greet us. I didn't know horses were magical, but what do I know? I walked up to the edge of the fence and held my palm out for the horse to approach on their own. This was something I'd seen the Goblin herders in my tribe do.

The horse walked up to me and lowered its head to me. Success! I slowly approached its head with my hand and began scratching. I felt something rough beneath my hand, so I shifted my scritches in a way that moved its mane off the area. I saw what looked like a jagged bone in the middle of its head. That made more sense. This must be a unicorn with a broken horn. I know those are magical!

I held up both hands so the unicorn could see I wasn't doing anything threatening and I climbed over the fence. I snapped my fingers over my shoulder to signal Gintina to raise up.

"Gintina, this is, well, this is embarrassing. I never got your name. Do you want me to just make one up for now?" I asked the unicorn. It shook its head. "Well, this is a unicorn that you will learn the name of later. It seems very nice, why don't you say hi?"

Gintina began to slink up my arm and slowly approached the unicorn. Gintina tilted her head when she reached the end of my arm and shyly flapped her wings. The unicorn looked cautious, but didn't make any sudden moves. That was probably good enough.

"You can get back in the bag now, Gintina. That was real good." I directed my attention back at the unicorn. "Do you want to show us around? We'd be really grateful."

The unicorn knelt down and offered its back to us. This was exciting! I hadn't ridden a horse, or a horse-like creature, since I was a teenager! I climbed onto its back and let it take the lead. It circled around the yard and ran towards the fence. It took a big leap and made it to the other side of the fence. This didn't feel like something I was supposed to do, but hey, I'm an adventurer. The rules don't apply to me.

The unicorn galloped along the edge of the fence until we reached a pond that was half inside the corral, half outside the corral. The horse let out a loud neigh. I think it was trying to tell someone something, but I had no idea if Gintina and I were the someones. It didn't take long to realize that it was something else. The water erupted, and we were showered with it. Gintina poked her head up from the bag to see what was going on. Another horse-like creature emerged from the pond. This one only really looked like a horse in its shape. If I weren't this close to it, I would probably think it was some kind of fish. It was green, covered in scales, and it had a blowhole on its head, like a dolphin. It cocked its head at us, and the unicorn knelt, putting Gintina and me at eye level with the sea-horse-thing.

"Hi! I'm Gin, and this is my friend, Gintina," I said, gesturing to the gwiber in my backpack. Gintina rested her head on my shoulder and rolled around on her back. I was pretty sure it was meant as some kind of greeting. "She's going to be moving here pretty soon, and I thought it'd be a good idea for her to meet everyone. Our unicorn friend here was showing us around. Do you have a name?"

The sea-horse thing lowered its head in a sort of nod.

"I figured. But you probably can't tell us, right? That makes sense. Well, it's nice to meet you. Is there anyone else in the water we should meet?"

It dove back into the pond, and the unicorn ran around to the other side of the pond. I didn't know if the unicorn was taking us somewhere else or if the sea-horse was getting someone else for us to meet. Before too long, the sea-horse poked its head back up, and a terrifying fish-cat kinda thing crawled out of the water. The unicorn made little circles with its head, probably in response to my sudden jump when I saw the cat thing. Its face was like any mountain lion I'd seen in the jungle, except it was bright blue. It also had paws and claws like a large cat, but its torso was much longer, almost like a serpent. There were shiny brown horns, the color of copper, poking out of its head. It opened its mouth to show its fangs. Even I knew this creature wanted to attack us. The sea-horse thing must have seen the fear in my eyes and swam around to the other side of it and splashed it with water. The water cat looked around and crept back into the water, like it forgot we were there.

"Remember that the water cat thing is pretty grumpy. I don't want you getting hurt," I advised Gintina.

The unicorn nodded in the direction of the sea-horse, and it nodded in response. The unicorn spun around and started galloping in a different direction. I turned around to wave at the sea horse thing.

"Bye! I'm sure Gintina will be seeing much more of you!"

The unicorn arrived at a wooded area. I could hear whistling above us. The trees were probably full of different kinds of magical birds. The unicorn knelt down again, probably suggesting we climb down. I obliged and wandered into the forest. Once I passed the first couple of trees, I saw that this was filled with way more than just birds. There were all kinds of winged creatures. I saw a winged lion that was missing claws pacing around a clearing. I saw small bunnies with large antlers hopping around. I even saw a couple of gwibers flitting around above us between branches.

"This must really be your new home, Gintina!" I exclaimed. Gintina wrapped herself around my neck like a scarf. I noticed that she did this when she was scared.

"I know. I'll miss you too, girl. But this is for the best. You should be with other animals like you!"

She buried her head under herself, trying not to face her reality. I recognized it because I used to do it all the time in the jungle.

"I know it's hard. Change is always hard. But look at Tilly! She thought she was really happy secretly taking care of you in that cave. But she is like a totally different person around Karuk."

Gintina lifted her head and looked me in the eyes. I think she was starting to understand.

"You'll love it here! You just have to get used to it."

She began to loosen herself from around my neck, but she still didn't move towards the treetops.

"I had a feeling someone was here. It's not like Trixie to jump out of the corral," an elderly-sounding voice emerged from behind us.

I turned to see it belonged to an old man that was some sort of person I'd never seen before. He looked kind of like if a bat turned into a person but still had some features like a bat. He had pointy ears on the sides of his head and an upturned nose. He also had leathery-looking wings connecting his arms to his back.

"Hi! I'm Gin. I don't think I've ever met anyone like you before. Is it rude to ask?"

"Of course not. If anything is true here on the reserve, it's that you should always ask about something you don't understand," the old man said kindly. "My name is Gael and I'm a Roedor. There's people like me all over Reyes, but what we don't often see are Goblins. You must have come with that group that Reggie brought in."

"I did! We brought my little buddy, Gintina, to find a place where she can be safe." I gestured to the winged snake around my neck.

"Oh, I've never seen a gwiber so attached to someone before. You must be great with animals. You wouldn't be looking for a job, would you? The reserve could always use more folks with an affinity."

"Sorry, me and my friends are adventurers. I never really thought of myself as good with animals, but I had an awful lot of fun playing my music for Gintina."

"That must be it! When gwiber get a little older than your Gintina here, they make songs with their wings. You probably reminded her of her mother."

I liked the sound of someone appreciating my music. Gintina was my first dedicated fan! I was going to miss her. "I'm glad I could give her some comfort on our journey. Can you help me get her to join the other gwibers up there? She's not wanting to leave me."

"Why don't you play some of your music? It might get the others to come down and join her."

I smiled and swung my drum around. I started beating out one of my favorite rhythms, and Gintina floated in front of me and started moving around like she was dancing. The other gwibers glided down from the trees and began dancing with her. It made me happy to see her making friends. As I finished playing, all of the gwibers, including Gintina, drifted up to the branches.

"That is mighty impressive, son," the old man told me.

"It's what I do," I answered.

"Well, you're very talented. If you ever get tired of adventuring, come back here."

I considered the way I felt right now. I felt really good that we were able to find Gintina a home where she could grow up with other gwibers like her. She was going to live a better life because we risked our lives to get her here. This must be how adventurers feel all the time!

I smiled back at the old man. "I'm pretty sure I'm meant to be an adventurer."

Chapter Nine

There are Elves Here?

Before we left the magic animal reserve, Reggie mentioned something about there being a portal to the Fey Realm in the adjacent island nation of Kapoor. We'd all heard the story about how oppressive and scary the Elves were. I'd heard all my life about the tragic history my Orc ancestors had suffered under them. But Gin, Dara, Tilly, and I were adventurers now, and we wanted to see something if it sounded interesting. Traveling to a different world sounded like something adventurers should do. We decided that since we didn't have anything pulling us in any specific direction, traveling to Kapoor in order to travel through the Fey Gate would be a pretty good next adventure.

We traveled to the port town of Manos and bought tickets for a ship headed to Kapoor. We used a bit of the money we'd gotten from the King of Valnan to pay for it. It felt really weird to be able to just pay for convenience. Before I realized we had money, I was preparing to craft another boat out of whatever we could find. It was a relief to be able to let someone else worry about navigating the ship while we traveled.

The ship docked in the city of Dhanri. I thought my tribe worked hard, but they had nothing on the people of Kapoor. I couldn't believe how fast they were unloading the ships. After disembarking, I was further shocked at the crowded streets. I had been to Anglachel a few times with the hunting party before, and Anglachel is a massive city, but I think that because there is so much of it, the streets never got this full. Everyone was moving with purpose. Everyone except the four of us. We had no idea where we were going.

"Where we headed, Dara?" Gin asked, looking up at Dara expectantly.

I noticed our group was starting to get its own rhythm. It was kind of comforting to have a sense of how we'd interact with each other, like a family.

"We've only just gotten here, Gin," Dara began. "I know about as much about this place as you do."

"I doubt that," Tilly said under her breath.

"There are Elves here?" I asked, surprised. I had never met an Elf before, but the streets were swarming with them. It was full of a mix of dark-skinned Elves and Humans. I didn't know if I should be terrified or curious.

"Well, yeah," Dara answered. "The nation of Kapoor was founded when the River Elves traveled to the Human and Mascara nation of Tag. The Elves began to work with the Humans and eventually pushed the Mascara out."

"What do you know? I didn't know that," Gin commented.

"O.K., O.K.," Dara relented. "If we're looking for a gate to the Fey Realm, we probably want to start with some kind of church. I know the River Elves essentially forced their religion on Humans by co-opting elements of their native culture. Most people actually don't know that."

"Gods, we don't need a history lesson," Tilly complained.

"So we need to find a church," I repeated.

"I bet that guy could take us to one!" Gin exclaimed, pointing at a man pulling a cart loaded with seats for passengers.

Gin raced up to claim the cart, but not before a finely dressed Elf sat in it before he could get there. It took us a few tries to actually get one, but finally, a muscular Human that couldn't have been over 18 years old agreed to take us to the closest temple of Pro'Va in what he called a rickshaw. He only spoke a handful of North Elven words, so communication was challenging. He raced us through the streets of Dhanri at a perfect speed to take everything in. There were shops set up all along the street, not unlike the market district in Anglachel. What was different were the bright colors. Clearly, the stall owners knew they had to stand out if they wanted to compete here, and that they did. Stalls would have elaborate tapestries serving as awning and drapes in reds, blues, and yellows scattered throughout.

It didn't take long, with the various smells wafting from food vendors, to remember that it had been quite some time since we'd eaten a proper meal. Once the young man dropped us off at a tall, multi-level temple, we took a quick break to pick up some street food. An older Human man was manning a stall beside the temple. He had two giant pots on either side of him. He also didn't speak much of the common language, but he did understand once we showed him a few pieces of gold. He scooped out some orange rice from one pot and an assortment of meat and vegetables, with a similar orange hue, into a magically created bowl. This is similar to the street food in Anglachel. You had to eat it within an hour, or the food would spill everywhere when the bowl disappeared. One bowl looked like enough food for all four of us. We gave him three pieces of gold and sat down on the curb of the street.

Gin was the first to grab a bit of it, and immediately regretted it.

"Ahhhhh!" He wailed. "Hot, hot, hot, hot. . . .!"

He wasn't stopping until someone helped him. Dara pulled out a stone he'd collected from a river in The Jungle and chanted the word "Riwante." He raised his hand that wasn't holding the rock over Gin's mouth, and water poured out of it. Gin drank and began to calm down.

"It is really spicy, guys," Gin finally said.

"I think we figured that out already," Tilly teased.

We all tentatively dug in, and it was incredibly spicy. The food I ate growing up often contained chilies, but it did not have this level of heat. However, once we got past the heat, the flavors were rich and something totally unique. We eventually finished all of the meal and sat the soon-to-be disappearing bowl on the curb before heading into the temple.

The temple itself was made of stone and shaped like a pyramid. It was as tall as some of the tallest trees in The Jungle. We walked through the door and were blown away. It was beautiful. There was a tiled floor creating an interwoven intricate pattern. There were clear pillars carved from some sort of crystal. It looked magical. An

Elven clergymanwearing a long, draping orange robe, approached us and began speaking in the same language everyone else had been using. He must have been able to tell from the looks on our faces that we didn't understand. He lifted his hand and pointed one finger to the sky, and performed a circular motion.

"Karana," he said. "Now, that's better. You can understand me now, yes?"

"Yes, we can!" Dara exclaimed. "That was a translation spell, and you did it like it was nothing. You must be really skilled!"

"I simply channel the essence of Pro'Va, the god of the natural world," he said.

"Father, I had heard of a god named Kawma," I said. "I was told he was the god of nature. Is there more than one?"

"Child, the domains of the gods are not as clear cut as everyone thinks," he advised. "But yes, the god you know as Kawma is one and the same as Pro'Va. Different lands have different names for the divine. And I am no priest. Here my parishioners call me swami. Why are you here?"

"We want to travel to the Fey Realm! We heard there was a gate here," Gin answered.

"Ahh, so you are pilgrims," the swami said.

"Yeah! That's it!" Gin quickly replied before any of us could contradict him.

"That explains your interesting collection of people. It is truly rare to see an Orc and a Goblin here," he said.

"We just love Kawma so much! We want to honor him," Gin lied convincingly.

"It is an honor to welcome you. I have tools for you," the swami said.

He supplied us with a map and gave each of us something he referred to as a sacred seed. Apparently, it is traditional for pilgrims of Pro'Va to plant these seeds on the other side of the portal. It sounds to me like an excuse for members of the church to do work for the River Elves.

With the map, the portal wasn't actually that hard to find. I took the lead, and Dara helped to figure out anything I couldn't. Eventually, we made it to a river that was marked on the map as the River Sayanna. All that was left to do was follow the river upstream. It started in the city and moved into a much more open green space. We could see houses in the distance that clearly indicated the rural part of Kapoor. Eventually, the river lead us to an outcropping of trees. These trees looked harder, sturdier than the trees I was familiar with in The Jungle. I was used to seeing the ground covered in vines and various flowers, this was all green grass. As we walked into the forested area, it was subtle at first, but became clear that all of the plant life was becoming progressively more dead. We saw a grouping of black husks of trees that grew together in an arch shape.

"I think that was the gate," Dara said.

"This doesn't feel right," I said. "Everyone stay on guard. I don't know what is going on here."

"I don't know if whatever caused this is still here," Tilly said. "Listen, this place is as quiet as a graveyard. And kinda looks like one, too."

"It could be something spiritual, but I don't sense any presence here other than us," Dara observed.

"So I guess we're not going to the Fey Realm," Gin sighed.

"Is there anything we could do?" I asked Dara.

Dara squinted in thought. "Maybe. At Arcana University, I read about this spell that could transfer life from one creature to another. It was something used by really dark wizards to steal life from children and stuff. But maybe we can use it here."

"You're not giving my life to these trees," Gin said. "I don't care how cool the Fey Realm is."

"No, I think we are carrying children," Dara said.

"The seeds!" I realized.

Dara nodded. "Yes, I think I might be able to transfer the potential life of the seeds into the trees that form the archway."

"So what do we do?" Gin inquired.

"Just give me your seeds and some time," Dara said.

Dara spent the next hour drawing an intricate magic circle in the dirt in front of the archway. He then drew a diamond design over top of the entire circle. He placed one seed at each point on the diamond. He then carefully walked into the center of the circle and took a deep breath.

"You've got this!" Gin encouraged.

"I hope so." Dara shrugged. "I've never tried to channel anything this powerful before."

"We're here if you need us," I reminded him. "We'll rush in if it looks like things are going bad."

"Thanks, that actually helps," Dara said. "O.K. , everybody ready? I'm not entirely sure how this will play out."

"C'mon, Dara, you're a bleedin' genius," Tilly said.

Dara extended his arms out on either side of his body, and his hands began to glow with a sickly green light. Then he started to chant.

"Reseverne Forcineri Consumé. Reseverne Forcineri Consumé. Reseverne Forcineri Consumé!" He finished by raising his voice to a shout and slamming his hands onto the ground below. The green color extended from his hands and touched each of the seeds. The glow became brighter and brighter until it was hard to look at. Finally, the color raced back along the diamond shape back into Dara's hands. But this time, it wasn't just his hands that were glowing; it was his whole body. His face shifted to an expression of brief panic, then realization. He dashed to the archway and threw his hands in the middle, where the portal would be. The green drained from his body and seeped into the ground below. Color began to return to the trees that composed the arch. They began to regrow leaves and even bloom orange flowers. Dara stepped back, and the space between the arch began to shimmer and took on a silvery hue.

"You did it, Dara!" Gin exclaimed. "You saved the portal!"

"I did," he said, his voice indicating a hint of disbelief. His body began to sway and fall towards the ground, but not before I could run up and catch him.

"You O.K.?" I asked.

"Yeah, just a little tired. We should probably go through the portal now. I don't want to have to do that again," Dara suggested.

"We really doin' this?" Tilly asked.

"We are," I confirmed. "We're adventurers."

Chapter Ten

Can You Believe We're Going to Save the World?!?

I HAD NEVER WALKED through a portal before. When I was really young, the Hukawan tribe had an incredibly old shaman that could use spatial magic. He would use it to visit other tribes deeper into the jungle. So I know that there are people that can use spatial magic to teleport and create portals, but I was never sure what really happened when you walked through it. Was it really you that passed through to the other side, or a magical copy? How would we even know? I knew that I basically accepted that none of those concerns mattered when I ran off with Gin and Dara to become an adventurer. Using magic to travel is just part of the gig.

I didn't know what to expect the Fey Realm to look like, but I definitely did not expect it to remind me so much of home. The ground was covered with plant life, and we were surrounded by trees, except for a humble dirt path leading deeper into the forest. I wasn't really sure what to do next. Were we just looking around? Now that we've done it, are we pretty much done now? I looked to Dara so I could follow his lead.

Dara was still stumbling, but began shambling forward down the path. I followed him without looking back because I knew Gin and Tilly would be close behind. I still didn't know where we were going, but I didn't have to wonder for long. The clearing opened up into a large settlement nestled in the trees. As soon as we emerged from the forest, an older Elven woman with dark skin ran up to us.

"Do you have word of the other side? What is happening?"

"We came here as part of a pilgrimage," I said, continuing our cover.

Her face told us that she was very worried. "We haven't seen anyone from the other side in weeks. We were worried something happened."

"You may be right about that," Dara began. "The portal gate wasn't working. All the trees and grass around it were dead. I was able to bring it back to life with my magic, but I don't know what caused it."

"He's trying to cross to the other side," she said cryptically.

"Who is he?" Tilly asked.

"As pilgrims, you must know that Pro'Va isn't truly the god the people of Kapoor worship. We all worship the Fey god, Sayanna. Sweet Sayanna was the one who granted Elves our great magic power. The seasonal courts forget, but we of the River remember," she said reverently.

"So this Sayanna is trying to come to Galevyn? That doesn't sound so bad. You just called her sweet," Gin concluded.

"Oh, were it just Sayanna I was referring to! You see, her brother, Puché has always been jealous of her. We should have seen this coming. Once we convinced the Humans to perform rituals to honor Sayanna, of course Puché would desire to cross over and destroy your world."

"Destroy? I don't like the sound of that," Tilly said.

"Nor should you," the Elven woman agreed. "We of the River have built a life utilizing both sides of the portal. It would be challenging to return to only utilizing our limited space in the Fey Realm."

"I'm sorry, who are you?" Dara said, a little frazzled. "This is a lot to take in. I've always learned there were eight gods. Every child in Anglachel knows that. And each god rules over a different domain of magic. That's just how it works. And you're telling me that Kawma was a different god all along?"

"Forgive me, young ones, my name is Sitara. I am the elder on this side of the gate." she said, introducing herself. "I do not know of this Kawma you speak of. We simply convinced the Humans of Kapoor to honor their god, Pro'Va, with rituals meant for our Sayanna. I do not know if Pro'Va or this Kawma you mention is real. I have my doubts based on what we know about the knowledge of those on your side of the gate. But Sayanna and Puché are both very real. Sayanna has continued to support us in your realm, now it appears Puché hopes to oppose us."

Well, that explanation was a mixed bag. I'm sure Dara was following it, but all I got was she called everyone from Galevyn stupid and thinks our gods are fake. But if there is a real threat against our home, someone had to do something. And are we adventurers, or are we adventurers?

"We have to help. What can we do?" I asked.

"Come with me. I have the supplies you will need to defeat Puché. He is likely posing as another god, much like our arrangement with Sayanna. However, his dark machinations are not meant for mainstream consumption. He likely has far fewer followers or at least many smaller sects. One of these must be gaining power. I imagine they would appear to you as an extremist cult to one of your world's other gods," she finished.

"Do you have any idea where we would even start?" Tilly said as we began to follow her.

"This I do know. Once the portal stopped functioning, I scryed on your world to see if there were any large collections of magic that would be associated with Puché. I found a heavy concentration of necromancy on the northeastern coast of the land your people refer to as Daragon," she said.

"Necromancy?" Dara said thoughtfully. "They must be posing as a Quietus cult."

"At least we're close to Daragon. I'm sorry, but does no one else feel really excited? Can you believe we're going to save the world?" Gin stated.

"I sure hope so, Gin," I replied.

Chapter Eleven

Trust Me. I'm Weird.

Dara

How long does this friggin' desert go on for?" Gin grumbled.

His small goblin body was not used to the dry heat of Daragon. I was happy to be here. We'd already journeyed through the jungles of Anglachel, the mountains of Ferreira, and the marshlands of Kapoor. The deserts of Daragon was one of the last two distinct geographic regions of Galevyn I had to check off my bucket list. We were so close to being able to say we'd literally traveled across the planet.

"We should be there any minute now," Karuk reassured him.

"You told him that an hour ago," Tilly reminded her. "Are you sure you're reading that map right?"

"I know what I'm doing," Karuk insisted.

"I trust her," I said.

"Why don't you make sure, Dara," Gin whispered loud enough for Karuk to hear.

"Yeah, you could make sense of this complex geography," Tilly commented sarcastically, gesturing to the miles of desert around us.

I hated being the smart one. I trusted Karuk's instincts. She knew how to guide us through Hell itself. I could trust her to get us through a desert. I didn't like being the one my companions relied on to check her work.

I walked up to her and took a look at her map. As far as I could tell, the map matched up to the place that we currently were. I mean, a blank desert looks like a blank desert, whether it is in person or on a map.

"We seem to be on the right track," I reassured them.

The sighs from Tilly and Gin were audible. What could I tell them? Walking through a desert is boring. It is big and it takes a while to get through. I don't know what they expected. Karuk turned her head towards me and gave me an approving smile, her Orc tusks creeping over her mouth. I gave her a knowing nod and settled back to my spot into the middle of our party.

"I hope the lead we got from that old woman was right. I'd hate to be sweating through my favorite pair of travel pants for nothing," Gin complained.

"What an intriguing thought," Tilly snapped. "I'm certain no one else among us has had a similar thought."

"I'm just trying to keep my mind off this heat," Gin explained. "Let's talk about something. What do you got, Dara?"

"What?" I asked, surprised.

"Come on, buddy. You're always wanting to talk about your magic stuff. This is your chance. You've got a fully captive audience," Gin suggested. Tilly let out a choked laugh.

I didn't know where he was getting this. I wasn't going around trying to talk to them about my magic. I was just always thinking about magic and sometimes my thoughts found their way out of my mouth. I'd always presumed they understood that. Then again, I don't think that ever escaped my thoughts.

"Do you really want to hear about the nuanced differences of fire and lava magic?" I asked, hoping the idea of it would bore him into accepting silence.

"Please, no heat talk," Gin pleaded. "Maybe you can talk about, like, ice and water magic. Is that a thing? Maybe the thought of it would cool us off."

"I can see your thought process, but it is very different. Ice and water magic are actually both water magic," I said.

"Great!" Gin said, "Keep going. That works for me."

"I don't know if the magic talk will keep me entertained," Tilly spoke up from our flank, "but the show the two of you are putting on is pretty great."

Karuk laughed from up front.

"Now, you need to keep paying attention to where we're going," Tilly chastised.

"Tilly, you know I could do this in my sleep," Karuk reassured her. "We just have to keep going northwest until we run into a savannah."

"Right! The famous Savannah of the Dragon. I don't know how I could have forgotten it," I exclaimed.

"What are you going on about now?" Gin asked.

"That blasted list of his," Tilly said. "He wants to travel to all the interesting places in Galevyn."

"Did I know that?" Gin said.

"Probably not," Karuk said. "You're always too busy listening to yourself talk to hear anybody else."

"Did you say something, Karuk?" Gin asked. Gin let out his mischievous giggle, while Karuk chucked a pebble over her shoulder and hit Gin squarely in the head. "Hey Karuk!" he chided. "Where did you even get a pebble? It's been desert and sand ever since we got to Daragon."

"I hung onto one from Kapoor," Karuk said matter-of-factly.

Gin shook his head. "You're so weird."

"Hey, that's my girlfriend," Tilly playfully snapped.

"That doesn't mean she's not weird. If anything it probably makes her more weird. An Orc dating a Gnome? Come on, it is a little weird," Gin said.

"Says the singing Goblin," Karuk retorted.

"Sure. We're all weird," Gin said. "No one is denying that. I was just commenting on your specific brand of weirdness."

"It's why we work together," I suggested.

"You're not that weird," Tilly commented. "You're just a Human who studied magic. The weirdest thing about you is that you chose to hang out with us."

"Trust me, I'm weird," I assured them. "I'm a Human that dropped out of Arcana University because he thought he was smarter than the teacher. I'm a Human who always talks to himself but has trouble talking to other people."

Gin considered this. "That's just socially awkward."

"Welcome to weird for Humans!" I exclaimed. "Trust me, I was the guy in school that everyone pointed at and said 'That guy's weird!'"

"Humans are the worst," Tilly said. "Present company excluded."

"You'll hear no arguments from me," I agreed.

"Look alive, folks," Karuk barked from up front. "Monster ahead."

"What are we looking at?" Tilly asked.

Gin looked all around. "I don't see anything."

"It just went underground. There's a sand wyrm ahead, I think it's headed our way," Karuk explained.

I combed through my brain to figure out what would work well against a sand wyrm. It attacks its prey by pulling them underground. That's it! I pulled out my spell component pouch and grabbed a crystal and began twirling it between my fingers.

"Alright guys, get ready to jump. Things might get a little chilly," I warned.

Gin pumped his fist into the air. "Sweet!"

I channeled my magic energy into the crystal until I could see it leave small bits of frost as it twirled. I slammed my hand into the sand and said the magic words. "Iceslo Comformum!" I screamed.

My companions jumped into the air as a thick sheet of ice began to cover the sand below us. I quickly pulled my hand away before it could get frozen in place. Just as my spell finished, we heard a loud thump. Fissures began to form in the middle of the ice disc I'd just created.

"I coulda done that," Gin jested.

Tilly gave Gin a stink eye. "Shut up."

There was blood starting to show below the ice. We could also see the monster's teeth as it worked on chewing through the surface. Gin and I walked to the edge of the disc, and Tilly crouched down in front of us, getting ready to pounce. Meanwhile, Karuk drew her hand ax and stood ready by the creature's head. Gin began to pound out a rhythm on his drum and thin magical barriers began to form around each of our forms. I began digging through my component pouch, preparing my next spell. This wasn't our first fight.

Once we each got into position, the wyrm crashed out of the icy surface. Karuk slammed down onto it with her ax. Brown wyrm blood splashed up and coated her cloak. Tilly ran up to flank the beast and dug both of her daggers into the back of its head. The creature wailed in pain, but it wasn't finished yet.

It managed to push half of its body out of the hold and crunched down on Karuk. The kind of pressure it caused would normally kill an Orc of Karuk's size, but Gin's barrier magic held strong. The spell I wanted to cast called for glass shards, but I didn't have any in my component pouch. I looked around and realized there were basically tiny shards of glass all around us. I turned around and scooped up a handful of sand. I began chanting as I rushed up to the wyrm. "Frosto Consumae, Frosto Consumae, Frosto Consumae."

I plunged my hand into the open wound Karuk's ax had created and released the sand. Frost began to spread throughout the creature's body. Its eyes began to freeze over as its life came to an end.

I went over and pulled Karuk down from the dead wyrm's mouth.

"You o.k.?" I asked.

"Yeah, great. I feel exhilarated!" she exclaimed.

"I've never seen that spell before," Tilly said. "Is that new?"

"A little," I said. "I just adapted an ice attack spell to create an aura and . . ."

"Please don't go on again," Gin said.

We all laughed. Karuk sliced off a chunk of the creature and built a fire to turn it into jerky. I cast a fire spell to dispose of the rest of the corpse. After a short break, we continued our journey.

"How much longer, Karuk?" Gin asked.

"We should reach the savannah any minute now," she replied.

"I swear you said the same thing an hour ago," Tilly complained.

I smiled to myself and started thinking about what we'd find at the Savannah of the Dragon. I was going to have to start a new list.

Acknowledgments

Thinking about acknowledgements for this book made me think a lot about everyone that I have ever referred to as a "best friend." I feel like we throw that term around. Best friend becomes more of a tier than a person. I don't know about anyone else, but there is definitely someone in my life that is my #1 person. The person that I know will always be there if I need them.

I knew Dustin in high school, but we really weren't friends until college. The transition to college is always challenging, but it is easier when you have someone to go through it with. Dustin was that for me. We always had separate friend groups, we always had our own things going on, but we always came back to each other at the end of the day.

This publishing journey never would have happened with Dustin. He's the one that encouraged me to just go for it. I hope everyone has that one person that pushes them, and I hope I've been able to pay you back for all you've done with my friendship. Thanks for everything.

About the Author

Terry Bartley is the founder and creative director of Starlight King Press and a journalism, literature, and English teacher at Scott High School. He is the host of Most Writers are Fans, a podcast about the intersection of writing and fandom, and Ink Over AI, which explores how writers can engage ethically and responsibly with AI without outsourcing their creativity. His work has appeared in the Coal Valley News and Screenrant.

He has won awards for writing and broadcasting from the West Virginia Associated Press, the National Broadcasting Society, and MarCom. He has a B.A. in English from the University of Phoenix and an M.A. in English Education from Western Governor's University.

He loves tabletop roleplaying games, reading comics, and watching TV shows starring complicated women. He lives in rural West Virginia with his dog, Etsy.

His debut novel, Destined for Greater Things will debut in Summer 2026.

Thanks

If Karuk's story meant something to you, Gin would probably say that's worth celebrating, quietly, so you don't get caught. Ruki would tell you to leave a review on Amazon or Goodreads. It genuinely makes a difference for indie authors.

Twitter: *@terrybartley*
TikTok: *@terrlet*
Instagram: *@terrlet*
Facebook: *@terrybartleywriter*
Podcast: *Most Writers Are Fans*

Destined for Greater Things

Coming Summer 2026

Karuk

I STILL COULDN'T BELIEVE it. They were all gone. Gin, Dara, even Tilly. I wasn't supposed to do this on my own. "We never leave each other." That's what me and Gin always said. But I left them. I left my best friend, my girlfriend, and, well, Dara.

I couldn't get Dara's look of desperation out of my mind when he begged me to leave and find help. His chestnut blonde hair was matted with blood, his rectangular glasses cracked all to hell, and he was the last of my friends to hang onto consciousness as the final bits of oxygen within the forcefield they were trapped within filled his lungs. "Get out of here, Karuk! This is too big for us. Find Dean Constance at the University. He'll know what to do!"

I didn't want to leave my friends magically trapped in an ancient shrine of the Death Cult, but I couldn't help them by myself. Their best chance was me leaving, even if it broke my heart to do it.

It took everything in me to remember Dara's nerdy Human face, which was typically scrunched up in concentration, trying to solve one of Galevyn's many mysteries. Gin would know what to say to keep me motivated. His tiny Goblin frame held enough enthusiasm for a man three times his size. And Tilly. Tilly would give me someone to hold when everything was falling apart. Her tiny Gnome hands somehow fit perfectly into my enormous Orc ones.

I stood against the railing of the ship, staring at the ocean in the direction of Daragon. The last place I saw my friends alive. No, they're still alive. They have to be. That's why I'm here. To get help, and return to save them.

I could have been standing here for a few hours or a few days. I couldn't tell anymore. I didn't even notice whenever the ship docked. I jumped when I felt a tentative tap on my shoulder.

"We're here, miss."

Even though I left my tribe and Anglachel to become an adventurer, the people here were still scared of me. Unfortunately, some things never change.

I turned to face the cautious crewman. An average-sized human man with light skin and sandy blonde hair. "Thank you."

He nodded but looked like he still had something to tell me.

"Go on," I prodded.

"I'm sorry, miss. As you are an Orc, we are required to escort you to Angalchel customs."

I'd never actually done this part before. I left Angalchel from The Jungle. I knew that Orcs were typically only allowed within the city as part of larger trading parties. Of course, there would be some procedure for those returning through the city to ensure we don't just run around it freely.

I took a deep breath. "Fine. Take me where I need to go."

While remnants of fear remained on his face, he did incline his head into something of a modest apology.

He led me through the docks, to the best-looking building among a string of shoddy warehouses. It used finer wood in its construction, with the crest of the

Anglachelean royal family carved into the door. I always found the crest funny in a morose sort of way. It showed a merchant shaking hands with a king. It was supposed to symbolize how Angalchel was all about equality and how a merchant was supposed to have the opportunity to rise to the same economic standing as royalty. I could remember coming into the city with trading parties as a child. We were essentially merchants, and yet I had to be escorted here because I couldn't be trusted to walk through the city unchecked.

The room itself was pretty small. The walls were lined with filing cabinets, and there were a few desks in the middle of the room turned to face the entrance. Only one desk actually had somebody behind it. He was a finely dressed human with red hair and freckles. He looked young but not too young, probably in his 40s. There was a name placard on the edge of his desk that said "Mr. Louis."

His face scrunched up in confusion when he saw me. "What do we have here?"

I had been in Anglachel enough times to know that when dealing with authority, you let the officials do the talking for you if it avoids conflict. I stood quietly and looked at the ship's crewman.

He eventually took the hint. "Yes, sir. This is an adventurer named—" he checked his notes. "Karuk. She has just gotten off our ship inbound from Daragon."

"I didn't know they had Orcs in Daragon," Mr. Louis considered out loud.

"It doesn't, generally," the crewman acknowledged. "But we do get adventurers passing through from all over."

Mr. Louis finally looked at me. "Are you from the Jungle of Despair?"

"Yes, sir. I'm from the Hukawan tribe." I kept my response brief.

"Right, their hunters pass through here sometimes. What brought you to Daragon?"

"I need to seek help from Arcana University. I would greatly appreciate it if I could be allowed to pass through the city to reach it."

"Of course, we would just need to fill out the paperwork. Then we can sign you up for a safe bracelet."

"Safe bracelet?" I inquired. I'd never heard of them.

"Yes, a safe bracelet. If an Orc or Goblin has a safe bracelet on, that tells the guards that they have been approved to walk the city freely." He held up a thick leather bracelet with a large blue crystal affixed to the center. "They can even scan the crystal to ensure it is the real thing."

This felt incredibly condescending. I wanted to get mad, but I also didn't want to confirm all the stereotypes about Orcs this city has. I took a deep breath, finding my inner calm. "That should be fine."

"Great, so that will just be a 2,000-gold fee for the bracelet, and we can get you on your way, Miss Karuk."

I felt my eyes instinctively widen. 2,000 gold? I have most of the money we made adventuring, but there wouldn't be much left after this. I was hoping to use that gold to pay for additional help in case saving the world wasn't enough of a reason to join me.

"Perhaps I could be escorted to the University. That is truly the only place I need to go," I suggested.

"I'm sorry, ma'am, but the only place the guards would be allowed to escort you is back to The Jungle of Despair."

"Back to The Jungle? I didn't even come from The Jungle this time." I could feel myself starting to lose my temper despite myself.

"There is no need to raise your voice, Miss Karuk. The guards could also escort you to the dungeons if you'd prefer," Mr. Louis somehow said very calmly.

They weren't giving me any choice. Clearly the only Orcs they can trust in the city are those that are willing to be extorted. This was legal robbery.

"Very well," I finally said, pulling out my coin purse. "I'll pay the 2,000 gold pieces."

"Thank you for your cooperation," Mr. Louis said.

www.ingramcontent.com/pod-product-compliance
Lightning Source LLC
Chambersburg PA
CBHW062217150726
47991CB00006B/2316